Love is Beautiful Book 2

New Adult Sweet Romance Series, Volume 6

Ellie J. Adams

Published by Wheelhouse Publishers LLC, 2020.

Copyright

Pittsfield, MA 01201
To learn more about Wheelhouse Publishers, visit:
wheelhousepublishers.com

Chapter 1

In spite of her exhaustion, Hunter insisted that Amber stay awake once they arrived in Paris.

"The jet lag will a lot worse if you take a nap," he warned her.

"I can't help it," she muttered, yawning sleepily as they waited to exit the plane.

She had slept fitfully during the flight, overwhelmed by the excitement of traveling and knowing that she was going to be living in France.

Fortunately, her adrenaline kicked in once they exited the custom's line and began walking toward the baggage area. She was finally here! Okay, so she was still in the airport. But still.

Amber bounced on her heels as they waited for their luggage to materialize. Her eyes widened as she saw a uniformed man holding up a sign with Hunter's last name printed in large, bold letters.

"Is that you?" she asked, nudging Hunter.

"Ah! Great! Right on time!" Hunter waved the man over.

"Mr. Webb?" The uniformed man bowed slightly.

"Yes, thank you."

"Will there be additional luggage, sir?"

"Four suitcases. Plus these two bags," Hunter said, his tone courteous but not overly friendly.

"Very good, sir. I'll get a luggage cart."

The uniformed man nodded respectfully and walked away.

Amber stared at his retreating figure.

"Are you okay?" Hunter asked. "Something wrong?"

"Who is that guy?"

Hunter laughed. "Just a driver from a car service. No big deal."

"Isn't that a bit luxurious?" Amber murmured.

Hunter grew pensive.

"You know, I honestly never thought about it before," he admitted. "But my parents' company has always had a car service for guests."

He smiled and leaned down to kiss her forehead.

"I know it isn't as nice as a bus crammed with people. But I'll try to make it up to you."

Amber giggled. "You do that!"

She allowed Hunter to smooth away her discomfort. She should be happy that Hunter had this kind of money to splurge. So why did it feel so weird to her?

She had a flash of her mom sitting in the trailer in her faded robe and slippers, drinking from a can of cheap beer. Amber shivered. Was she ever going to escape her past? Was she really worth this type of attention?

"Are you cold? Here, take this."

Hunter pulled off his sweater and slipped it over her head.

The sweater was really too warm, but Amber smiled and squeezed Hunter's hand appreciatively.

Minutes later, the driver returned and stood silently a few feet away. Amber's first impulse was to start chatting with him. Would that be inappropriate? Was there some sort of secret rule book for how to act with people you paid to perform a service for you?

Finally, the luggage arrived and Hunter and the driver placed everything on the luggage rack. Hunter held her hand firmly as they navigated through the bustling airport and out into the street where the car was parked.

The air was frigid outside, but Amber was only outside a moment before the door was opened for her. She slid inside the relatively warm car, grateful that they didn't have to stand around waiting for public transport.

Hunter noticed her shivering and put his arms around her.

"Sorry, baby. I should have kept your coat out for you."

"That's okay," Amber said, snuggling against him. "I prefer you to any old coat."

"Good to know," Hunter said. "But I'll have the driver turn up the heat."

Tapping on the shield between the front and back, Hunter got the driver's attention. He spoke quickly in French. The driver nodded and smiled at Amber. In only a little while, the car was noticeably warmer.

"What time do we meet your parents?"

Hunter immediately looked at his watch.

"We have reservations at the hotel restaurant at one o'clock," Hunter said, his brow furrowing.

"So we should still have time to check in and freshen up before lunch."

"How dressy is this restaurant?" Amber stared down at herself in alarm.

"Don't worry, baby. I packed your new dress with my suits."

"Oh, thanks," Amber mumbled.

What was she getting herself into? She had one nice dress to impress two extremely wealthy parents. Her stomach felt queasy.

"Don't worry, gorgeous," Hunter murmured, pulling her close for a hug.

"They've got my good taste. They'll love you!"

The driver interrupted with a question in French. Amber had been trying to teach herself key phrases the last few days, but she couldn't keep up with the rapid speech. Now she felt completely out of place.

But when the car pulled up to a beautiful hotel, her mouth dropped open. She hadn't expected a dinky hotel of course. But this place exuded opulence. A porter rushed to open the door and greeted her with a warm smile.

"Bonjour, Mademoiselle."

"Bonjour," Amber mumbled back, blushing.

Hunter chatted for a moment with the porter in French before escorting Amber into the palatial lobby. He kept a protective hand against the small of her back.

"Our bags will get sent to the room," he said, guiding her to the front desk.

The gentleman at the front desk smiled at Hunter warmly and began speaking in rapid French. Amber only caught Hunter's name. She stood awkwardly, trying to blend in.

Finally, Hunter signed a register and led Amber away.

"Have you stayed here before?"

Amber tried not to gawk at the crystal chandeliers over her head or the enormous stone fireplace blazing in the lobby.

"Yes. Several times with my parents. The company uses it for business, so management always gives us great rates. I think that they upgraded us for free this time."

Hunter looked at her anxiously. "I hope you like it."

Amber couldn't help herself. She burst out laughing.

"What?" Hunter looked confused.

"Hunter, the nicest hotel I've ever stayed at was a chain hotel that had a mini fridge and microwave in the room. I have a feeling this is at least a tiny step up from that."

Hunter shook his head sadly.

"First, I had to compete with exhaust fumes from a local bus. Now, I have to worry about a chain hotel that featured a mini fridge and microwave."

Amber punched his shoulder. "Now who's being sarcastic?"

Hunter rubbed his arm and grinned.

The elevator dinged and Hunter moved quickly, holding the door open as an elderly woman disembarked. He waved Amber inside with a flourish of his hands. They had the elevator to themselves.

Hunter punched the button for their floor.

"You don't need to be nervous," he said. "My parents are going to love you."

"I feel out of place," Amber admitted.

"Gorgeous, you look amazing. And my parents are down to earth in spite of having tons of money."

As Hunter finally opened the door to their room, Amber forgot about her anxieties.

"Oh! Wow!"

She stared in amazement, trying to take in everything at once. This was not a hotel room. It was more like an apartment.

The living room alone was larger than the hotel room she had once stayed in.

On one table stood an enormous vase of fresh flowers, a bucket with a bottle of champagne, and a wicker basket stuffed with fresh fruits and assorted chocolates. A magnificent bay window, draped in elegant curtains, showed the bustling street below. The long sofa was a rich, white leather. The chairs were ornate with lovely fabrics and airy pillows. Attention had even been given to the lush carpet on the floor. Amber felt like she was Cinderella entering the palace.

"Nice, isn't it?" Hunter asked.

Was this typical for him, Amber wondered. Was this the type of luxury he was accustomed to every time he traveled?

"I feel under dressed," Amber finally said, when she felt as though she could speak.

"You look good wherever you are, gorgeous," Hunter said, swooping her in his arms and kissing her gently on the mouth.

"Oh, goodness! I need a shower!" Amber said, remembering that she was meeting Hunter's parents in less than an hour.

Hunter laughed.

"Why don't you go first? Pick which bedroom you like the most. I'll meet the porter when he comes up with our bags."

Amber stepped into the first bedroom. Though not large, it featured a full bed with an elegant pale blue bedspread, a wing-backed chair, and an antique armoire. When she opened the top door of the armoire, she discovered a flat screen television tucked neatly inside. The bottom held roomy drawers. Long, luxurious silk drapes framed a large window that looked over the street below. Amber peeked out quickly before pulling the curtains shut for privacy.

A quick look into the other bedroom revealed a similar setup. The only difference was a more masculine pattern on the bedspreads and curtains. Also, instead of a window, one wall was completely covered by a flat screen television. She would let Hunter have this one.

Going back into the first bedroom, Amber kicked her shoes off. She padded into the impeccable bathroom. There was marble everywhere, including the floor. A vase of fresh flowers sat on the wide counter top.

She turned on the water, happy to see a full burst of water from the shower head. She chose shampoo and conditioner samples from an ornate wire basket. Mm . . . They smelled heavenly. She grabbed a bar of soap and placed everything on the silver tray beside the tub. Dropping her travel clothes on the floor, she stepped into the steaming spray.

Ah! There was almost nothing that compared to a hot shower. She could have stayed in there forever, but she was conscious of the time. She reluctantly finished quickly, stepping out and wrapping a thick towel around her. Even the towels were luxurious. She had no idea a hotel towel could be this soft and fluffy. She wrapped another towel around her hair in turban fashion.

As she started to leave the bathroom, she spotted robes and slippers behind the door. Even better! The slippers were way too big for her small feet, but they were so comfy that she kept them on and shuffled out of the room with the robe cinched at her waist.

"The shower's all yours!" Then she realized that Hunter was in the closet.

"Sorry to yell. I thought you were still in the living room."

"The porter came up right after you got in the shower. I sent him down with my suit and your dress for a quick pressing."

Hunter stashed her suitcases in the corner of the closet.

"Oh, I need those before you put them away."

Hunter pointed to the bottom half of the armoire.

"Your folded things are in the drawers."

"You unpacked my things?" Amber stared at Hunter.

Hunter shrugged. "I had time so I unpacked everything. Don't you do the same when you travel?"

Amber thought of how she normally yanked out what she needed during a trip and stuffed everything back in the suitcase at the end.

"Um . . . Yeah . . . Thanks for saving me the trouble."

Hunter chuckled.

"What?" Amber asked.

"I was joking when I suggested you unpacked your things."

Amber put her hands on her hips.

"How would you know what I do on trips?" she asked, annoyed.

She knew she wasn't the most organized person on the planet. But he didn't have to make fun of her.

"I'm sorry, baby," Hunter said, trying without success to erase the smile on his face.

"But you're hands down the sloppiest person I know."

"That's a terrible thing to say!"

Hunter folded his arms across his chest.

"Really? And I suppose it's nice for you and Caleb to joke together about me being a control freak?"

Ouch! Had Hunter overheard them?

"Well, you need to be a gentleman no matter what I say."

She turned and flung open the drawer to start getting dressed.

He had individually folded every single pair of panties. Who did that? She remembered how she had wadded all her panties and bras in one giant pile of her suitcase. She blushed.

"Ah, baby, don't be sore," Hunter murmured, coming up and embracing her from behind. "You're the most gorgeous slob in the world."

Amber twisted around so that she was looking up into those shimmering green eyes. It was hard to stay mad at him.

"Well, I have to admit that you are the most handsome control freak in the world," she murmured.

Hunter kissed her hungrily.

Amber felt herself responding until she glimpsed the clock behind his back. She broke free from his lips.

"Yikes! I've still got to dry my hair."

Hunter reluctantly let her go and headed for the bathroom.

Chapter 2

"Don't worry about mom and dad," Hunter said for the third time. "I promise that they don't bite."

Amber sighed. "Yes, but what if they swallow me whole?"

Hunter laughed. "Seriously. You have nothing to worry about."

"What's their normal reaction to you bringing a girl over?" Amber asked, suddenly curious.

To her surprise, Hunter flushed and turned away, starting to fidget with his tie.

"I think that this is on crooked. Can you check?"

Amber reached up and adjusted the tie by about a millimeter. She was going to have to figure out a way to pry information from Hunter. Why was he acting embarrassed? Had something happened with the last girl? Had the girl embarrassed herself? Used the wrong fork at dinner? Spilled dinner all over herself?

"Breathe, Amber," Hunter said, taking her hand.

Leaning down, he kissed her gently on the lips.

"I'm glad you look so natural. Mom will be impressed. She doesn't like heavy makeup."

Amber forced herself to take a deep breath. She closed her eyes and forced herself to relax. When she opened her eyes again, Hunter was watching and waiting silently.

"Okay, Monsieur Webb," she said with a confidence she didn't quite feel. "Let's do this!"

As they walked to the elevator, Hunter talked to her about some of the specifics of the company. She was surprised to learn that Hunter's mother was starting a foundation for underprivileged girls.

"She wants to provide opportunities in the arts."

"That's incredible," Amber said.

Hunter looked embarrassed for a moment.

"What?" Amber asked in alarm.

"I hope you don't take this the wrong way. My mom wants to talk to you about working for the company as a part-time intern."

Amber beamed. "Really? That would be great!"

Hunter looked relieved. "I just didn't want you to think she was asking because of . . . um . . . your past."

The elevator stopped. Amber waited until they stepped out to confront Hunter.

"Is she asking because of my past?" she asked, narrowing her eyes at him as she crossed her arms over her chest.

"No!" Hunter said with a fierceness that startled her.

"I told her that I thought that you were incredibly smart and might have some good ideas."

Amber studied him for a full minute, watching his posture until she was certain he was telling the truth.

"Well then, Monsieur Webb," she said, linking her arm in his. "Let's not keep the parents waiting."

Amber was glad to see that the hotel restaurant was quite private and that nearly half the tables remained empty. At least she wouldn't have to worry about talking over loud conversations. As they were shown to their table, Amber tried to squelch her nerves. Fortunately, both Hunter's mom and dad had big smiles on their faces as they stood to greet them.

Amber was amused to see Mrs. Webb give her son a kiss on each cheek before engulfing him in a hug. She was impressed when Mr. Webb gave his son an equally warm hug. She waited, hoping that her palms were not too sweaty. There was no way she could wipe them on this dress.

"Mom and Dad, this is Amber," Hunter said, beaming at her. "Amber, this is my mom and dad."

"It's a pleasure to meet you both, Mr. and Mrs. Webb," Amber said, her throat dry.

"The pleasure is all ours, Amber," Mrs. Webb said, warmly taking Amber's hands in both of hers.

Tall and slender, Mrs. Webb wore her long, gray hair fashioned into a low bun behind her head. Her beautiful skin, the color of pale honey, looked clean and fresh. If she was wearing makeup, Amber couldn't see it. She wore a simple, navy, sheath dress that accentuated her long legs. Only her heels were surprisingly high. Other than her wedding band, a delicate watch, and tiny diamond studded earrings, she wore no jewelry. She exuded simple elegance.

"Yes, Amber," Mr. Webb echoed, also extending a hand. His light brown hair was cropped short and he had streaks of gray around his temples. Although he was dressed in an expensive suit, his manner was warm and laid back.

Amber breathed easier as they all sat down. Soon, she was in a deep conversation with Mrs. Webb about her foundation. Apparently, Hunter wasn't kidding when he said that his mom wanted to offer her a position.

"I have great ideas," Mrs. Web confessed. "But I just don't know young people that well."

She leaned in as though a conspirator.

"You might have noticed that Hunter is years ahead of his chronological age."

Hunter paused in his conversation with his dad. He arched an eyebrow at his mother.

"Really, mom. I can hear you. I'm only about a foot away."

Mrs. Webb simply laughed and Amber had to smile.

"So Hunter has always been responsible and level headed?" Amber asked with a grin.

Mrs. Webb raised her salad fork for emphasis.

"He came out of the womb, shook his little finger at the doctor in charge, and demanded to know how long the poor man had been practicing and where he got his degree."

Hunter blushed but chose to ignore his mother.

Mrs. Webb turned serious. "The world has changed so much since I was raising Hunter. And he matured so quickly. I see youngsters in the street today and have no idea what they might be thinking."

"I would love to help, but I'm not sure if I have the necessary experience," Amber said.

Mrs. Webb smiled. "Your honesty is refreshing. I need someone to help me plan things. Someone who isn't afraid to tell me if an idea is quite horrible. Do you think you could do that, dear?"

Amber grinned and squeezed Hunter's arm to get his attention.

"Your mom is asking if I have difficulty giving an honest opinion."

Hunter grimaced. "Amber has never been afraid to tell me what she thinks. Good or bad."

"How refreshing!" Mr. Webb declared. "Finally, someone who stands up to Hunter."

"Aw, come on! Is this bash your son day?" Hunter stabbed his salad with his fork.

"Oh, sweetie, you know we love you!" Mrs. Webb patted Hunter's cheek and turned to Amber.

"What a lovely girl you are. I'm glad that we've finally gotten a chance to meet you!"

Mr. Weber turned his attention to Amber and inquired about her studies.

Amber relished the attention, but she was now really curious about Hunter's past. She knew that he hadn't dated in awhile, but his parents seemed borderline ecstatic to meet her. Had they feared that he would be a lifetime bachelor?

Lunch was delicious, but Amber soon found herself fighting back yawns.

"Dear, I'm sure that Hunter already warned you. As dreadfully tired as you must be, try to stay awake until this evening," Mrs. Webb said, watching with concern.

Mr. Webb turned to his son. "Hunter, we have to get back to the office. Why don't you take Amber sight seeing? A little brisk air will help revive her."

After hugs and kisses, the Webbs waved them off.

Hunter smiled as they headed back to the elevator.

"They absolutely adored you."

Amber yawned and smiled sleepily.

"I'm glad. Look, do you think I could just put my head down for twenty minutes?" she pleaded. "I can't keep my eyes open."

"Sorry, but that's not going to happen. I have to keep you awake. I'm exhausted, but I've done this before. Plus, my body is kind of between time here and the States."

"Do we just wander around the city to stay awake?"

"Why don't we go shopping? If you're going to be working, you'll need at least a couple of pairs of slacks and tops."

Oh! Amber hadn't thought of that.

"I don't know how much money I have to spend on clothes."

"You can pay me back after you get your first check," Hunter said. "Come on. I know where you can get just what you need at a bargain price."

Huh? What did Hunter know about bargain shopping? But she didn't have time for further questions. She was already half jogging to keep up with his hurried steps. Well, there were far worse things than a day of shopping in Paris.

Chapter 3

"What's the rush?" Amber finally asked, as Hunter stopped in front of a clothing boutique.

"Sorry," Hunter said, opening the door for her. "I was afraid you might try to make a break and run back to the hotel."

"I still could," Amber said.

But she was happy to be out of the wind and the cold. Her ears were stinging and her nose had started to run. She rummaged in her purse for a tissue as a svelte girl approached them.

The shop girl appraised them both. She crinkled her nose in Amber's direction, but was all smiles as she greeted Hunter.

Back off, Amber thought. She took Hunter's hand and brought it up to her lips.

Hunter must have gotten the point because he put a possessive hand around Amber's shoulders. He lowered his head and kissed her briefly on the mouth.

The shop girl took a step back, pretending to be grabbing a blouse off a rack. She motioned for them to follow. When they reached the rear of the store, Amber noticed a leather sofa and several comfortable chairs positioned near a dressing room.

An older woman with a pleasant face greeted them. The other girl stalked off.

After managing one brief "bonjour" Amber had used up all her conversational French and let Hunter do the talking. Even though she knew a few halting phrases, these people talked entirely too fast for her to understand.

Finally Hunter turned to her. "Madame LeForte will help you get fitted. I told her the sort of office environment my parents have so she knows what is appropriate. If you don't like something or need to ask a question, I can translate for you."

As her eyes flitted to the clothing racks, Amber didn't see any price tags. She turned to question Hunter, but he was already seated on the leather sofa and flipping through a magazine.

The matronly woman smiled reassuringly and led Amber into the dressing room. After taking Amber's measurements with a cloth measuring tape, Madame LeForte gestured to a comfortable chair and left the room.

Amber sat gingerly, hoping that the woman had a good sense of taste. After wearing jeans most of her life, she had no clue what sort of business attire was considered professional. Especially here in Paris. She tapped her boot on the floor nervously, stopping abruptly as the woman returned pushing a metal rack of outfits.

A half hour later, Amber was impressed. Almost everything looked wonderful while also remaining, surprisingly, comfortable. For every outfit that Amber approved, Madame LeForte led her out to parade in front of Hunter. If she hadn't been so groggy from jet leg, Amber might have objected. The woman was sadly mistaken if she thought Amber had to have Hunter's approval.

Of course, maybe she did need his approval. Would he buy her something that he didn't like if he was spending his own money? Would she want him to? In spite of his assurances, she suspected he would never let her pay him back for the clothing.

One thing was for certain. She needed to learn French if she was going to feel like she was on equal footing again.

Fortunately, she didn't have to worry about arguing with Hunter over her selections. He seemed pleased with everything. Either that or he just wanted to be done. He did seem exhausted when he gazed up from his magazine. She grudgingly admitted to herself that she was probably being a little hard on him today. He had promised his parents to keep her awake.

After Amber settled on several outfits, Madame LeForte brought out several pairs of heels. Amber balked. She didn't mind wearing heels for a dinner out, but she had to draw the line somewhere for the sake of her feet. She pointed hopefully at her boots. After a moment, Madame LeForte smiled and held up a finger. When she returned, she offered Amber a beautiful pair of black dress boots with a sensible heel.

Amber fell in love immediately. She literally beamed at the woman as she put them on her feet. They felt incredible! She felt a pang of worry about the cost. Even with no price tag, she knew these were expensive. But there was no way she was leaving this store without those boots.

Seeing her smile, Madame LeForte grabbed Amber's hand and pulled her out to show Hunter. The woman spoke in rapid French as she gestured animatedly with her hands.

Hunter grinned and nodded. He gave the woman a warm smile and then subtly handed her his credit card. He was so smooth that Amber almost didn't see it happen. Madame LeForte walked over to a small desk in the corner to ring up the purchases.

"So you like the boots best of all, gorgeous? Madame LeForte said she has never seen such a happy customer."

Amber grinned happily. "They're awesome! It's funny, but I never knew I loved boots so much until I met you."

Hunter laughed. "That's my skill in life. I help the ladies discover their fashion sense."

Amber punched his arm. "Only one lady. And don't forget it!"

"This trip is really bringing out the aggressive side of you."

Hunter massaged his arm and grinned.

"Oh, please! That punch wouldn't have knocked out a fly!"

Madame LeForte reappeared with a receipt for Hunter to sign as well as several beautiful bags. After they left the shop, Hunter insisted that they go to a small café several blocks away. The brisk air was freezing, but it did help in sharpening her senses. It also made her move quickly in anticipation of getting somewhere warm.

Ducking into the small café, Amber was immediately transported to bliss by the heavenly smells of baked goods. She had been expecting sort of a coffee shop atmosphere. This place, however, was much fancier than that. They were seated at a small table covered with crisp white linens. An attendant took their coats and packages.

"I thought that we were just going to a bake shop," Amber whispered.

Hunter merely winked at her and spoke to the older gentleman waiting on them. She was glad that Hunter had explained that the word "garçon" used in old movies actually meant "boy" and that it was considered quite rude to refer to one's waiter that way.

"No menu?" Amber asked, puzzled when they were left sitting alone.

"I wanted to surprise you," Hunter said, looking a bit uneasy. "I'm sorry. I should have asked you first."

Normally, she would have been upset. As it was, did she really want to agonize over a menu right now? Truthfully?

She shrugged her shoulders, too tired to really care that much.

"I take it you've been here before?"

Hunter smiled. "My mom used to bring me here all the time when I was a kid. It was our special place."

Amber stared at him guiltily. Oh! He had brought her here to try to impress her. And she had almost yelled at him for being too controlling.

"Your mom is really nice. You were totally right about how I would feel about her."

They were momentarily interrupted as two porcelain cups and saucers were placed in front of them. The waiter disappeared for a moment, but returned almost immediately with an ornate silver tea pot from which he deftly poured steaming cocoa. He placed the pot in the center of the table. To one side, he placed a small bowl of thick whipping cream.

"Mademoiselle?" he asked Amber, indicating the cream.

"Oui. Merci," she managed to squeak out with a nod of her head.

The waiter gently placed a shiny dollop of cream on top of her steaming cocoa. Then he swiveled his body to face Hunter.

"Monsieur?"

Hunter nodded and then spoke several sentences in French that completely evaded Amber. How in the world was she going to learn this language?

Amber took a sip of the hot, sweet cocoa and groaned. The warmth immediately began to thaw her chilly body.

"Oh, this is so good! Your mom was a saint to bring you here," she murmured.

Hunter smiled broadly, clearly delighted that she found pleasure. He took a sip and gave himself a cream mustache. He used the tip of his tongue to lick his upper lip clean.

Amber grinned in amusement. She had never seen Hunter do that before. She wondered if it was a childhood trait that he subconsciously reverted to when he was here. She would have to remember to ask his mom about it later.

The cocoa was so good that Amber practically gulped it down. She tried to be ladylike, but it was so good! She wondered if it was bad etiquette to refill her own cup. She didn't want to ask Hunter and risk looking even more ignorant.

Fortunately, the waiter came back a few minutes later with a silver basket loaded with pastries. He placed them at the side of the table with a delicate pair of silver tongs. Seeing Amber's empty cup, he immediately refilled it, only glancing casually at her to ascertain she still wanted the heavenly whipped cream.

Amber was happy to see Hunter accept another cup of cocoa as well because she didn't want to look like a pig. Once the waiter left, Hunter pointed at the tray of delightful goodies, explaining each to her.

"That one has a raspberry filling and that one has dark chocolate," he said. "That one is kind of a honey and nut treat. That one has sweet cream on the inside."

Amber's mouth watered. "They all look so incredibly good."

"We're taking the leftovers home so you'll have an opportunity to try all of them."

Hunter placed one pastry on his plate and neatly cut it in half with a knife and fork.

"Do you want to try half of this one?"

Amber stared at the raspberry filling oozing onto the plate.

"I think it would be dangerous if you didn't share it," she said, licking her lips.

Hunter laughed. He scooped up half the pasty and deposited it on her plate.

"This is my favorite one," he said shyly.

Amber already had her fork halfway to her mouth. She put it back down.

"Are you sure you don't want the whole thing?"

Hunter smiled. "I'm sure they have more in the back. I want to see if you like it as much as I do."

Amber studied the morsel before placing it in her mouth. The pastry was light and flaky with a drizzle of dark chocolate on top. She put it in her mouth and moaned again as the slight bitterness of the dark chocolate melded with the sweet freshness of the berries. This was definitely no canned fruit filling!

She looked up to find Hunter staring at her with a glazed look in his eyes. His eyes always seemed to change with his moods. Now they were like a stormy sea.

"What?"

Had she done something wrong? She looked down to see that her napkin was placed firmly on her lap. She hadn't knocked any silverware off the table. She checked her fork. Yes, the same fork as Hunter was using.

And then, just as suddenly, Hunter snapped out of whatever had come over him. He shook his head as though to clear it.

"Sorry, I got lost in my thoughts for a moment. Are you still enjoying the pastry? Would you like to split another one?"

"I don't know. Is it possible to burst from a sugar high?"

"From this tiny bit of sugar? Nah! We're good."

Amber grinned.

"How much do you normally eat when you come here?"

Hunter tapped his chin and thought.

"I honestly haven't been here in years. But I think that my record was five cups of cocoa and three pastries."

"Oh, my goodness!" Amber laughed. "That sounds so unlike you."

"In my defense, I was about seven years old at the time. So, you know, that makes it acceptable."

"You must have bounced all the way home," Amber said and giggled.

Hunter smile. "I do recall a lot of running that afternoon."

"Well, I can't imagine besting your record, but I do think that we need to try that honey and nut pastry."

Amber reached for the dessert tray. But in the process she knocked off several pieces of silverware.

Mortified, she wondered whether to pretend it hadn't happened or whether she should pick it up. She whipped her head around, convinced everyone had witnessed her clumsiness.

Chapter 4

"It's okay," Hunter whispered. He casually squatted by the table and retrieved the forks and spoons.

"Nobody saw except me. The waiter is way over there and that couple to our right has no idea where they even are."

Amber peeked at the people in question and relaxed. An older couple were staring at each other and holding hands. Hunter was right. They were in their own little world. Actually, the café was remarkably empty considering the quality of the food.

"Where is everybody anyway?" Amber asked once her nerves had settled.

Hunter stuck the wayward silver on the side of the table. Then he divided the honey and nut pastry.

"In the spring and summer, this place would be packed with tourists all hours of the day. But the locals usually come earlier or later in the day. My mom brought me here after school a lot."

Amber took a tiny nibble of pastry. Her mouth exploded with the sweetness.

"When do you have to be back at work? I still can't believe how nice they've been about giving you time off."

Hunter nodded. "Yeah, they bent over backwards to make things work for me."

All the sugar from the cocoa and the pastries was making Amber's head buzz. For the first time all day, she felt close to clear headed. She knew it was temporary, but for now she was going to take advantage of it.

"So, you never got around to telling me what this new deal is you made with them."

Hunter shook his head.

"Let's talk about that later, okay? I don't have all the details worked out yet."

Amber sighed. "You keep saying to trust you. But I feel kind of on edge not knowing what the next several months are going to be like."

Hunter looked alarmed. "Are you changing your mind about being here with me?"

"Are you kidding me? What girl turns down an extended trip to Paris with her boyfriend?"

She patted Hunter's hand reassuringly.

"Isn't there a limit to how long I can visit? I thought I needed a visa."

Hunter shook his head. "As an American, you can stay without a visa for up to three months."

Amber was too hyped up on sugar to let the matter drop.

"But I feel like you might . . ."

"Might what?"

Amber came to her senses. She couldn't very well tell Hunter that she feared that he was going to want to stay here in France. After all, as a dual citizen, he had no limitations on how long he could stay. And where did that leave her?

"I'm just tired and not thinking straight. I just . . ."

"What? You might as well come out with it now."

Amber tried to think of a delicate way to say what was on her mind. Finally, she just gave up and blurted it out.

"I know that you haven't dated recently, but you're really smart and so handsome. So I figured you would have had your share of girls meeting your parents. And me, well, I'm so different and . . ."

Hunter held up a hand to stop her.

"You are the first girl I've ever brought home to my parents," Hunter said softly. "I never felt this way about anyone until I met you."

What? Seriously? Amber stared at him.

"Your mouth is open," Hunter informed her with his head lowered.

"I don't know what to say."

Hunter rubbed his forehead. "How about 'Thank you, Hunter, for being so open when I know that you hate to talk about your feelings.'"

Amber smiled. "It almost makes me want to take things easy on you."

Hunter grinned, his body visibly relaxing. "Is that right, Miss Holloway?"

"Almost. But not quite."

"I see." Hunter drained his cup of cocoa and shrugged.

"That's just as well because I have years worth of evasion techniques."

Amber rested both elbows on the table and cupped her chin. She stared at him with what she hoped was a ferocious look.

"Thinking about your own strategy, baby?"

Hunter was arrogant. Arrogant and handsome with that bit of hot chocolate sticking to his upper lip.

Stop staring at his lips!

"You don't think I have a strategy?"

"You? Organized enough to think this through from beginning to end?"

"Yes, me," Amber said, crossing her arms across her chest.

"Are you saying that I'm not capable?"

Hunter wiped his mouth with his napkin and folded it neatly across his plate. He took his time.

She smiled, wondering how he was going to get out of insulting her.

"Amber, I believe that you can do anything that you put your mind to do."

Amber stared at him. Hmm . . . A compliment that didn't answer the question directly. He was good at his.

"So I have a strategy?" she asked, pushing him further.

Hunter smiled. "I thought I just answered you."

"You very politely circled my question."

"Baby, I believe that you believe that you have a strategy and that you are confident in your ability to best me."

Amber rubbed her own forehead, trying to replay his comment back in her mind. So much for the sugar high. Her brain was too tired to keep up with his word play.

"Why are we even talking about this now?" she asked irritably.

Hunter raised an eyebrow. "I believe you brought up the whole interrogation, gorgeous. I'm just trying to save myself."

Amber laughed. She was starting to get a little punchy.

"Hey, don't start hyperventilating on me, baby," Hunter warned, looking a little panicked.

Amber felt her eyes tearing up. Oh, no! Not now!

"Take some deep breaths."

Hunter grabbed her hand while also calling for the waiter. After a few quick words in French, the waiter rushed back with the bill while Amber concentrated on her breathing. By the time they left the café, Amber was feeling better. The icy wind in her face certainly helped. She shook her head when Hunter suggested getting a taxi.

"I think walking is better," she said. "And I honestly think I might fall asleep once I stop moving again."

They walked slowly back in the direction of the hotel, stopping at several art galleries to glance at the paintings. Amber was exhausted.

Hunter rubbed his eyes like a little kid. Noticing her grin, he blushed and jammed his hands into his pockets.

The street signs and shops all began to blur. Even the constant murmurs of French no longer seemed strange. Finally, Hunter stopped at a small market and purchased fresh sandwiches and bottled water. They ate those slowly as they approached the hotel.

"Please tell me that we can go to sleep when we get back," Amber said wearily.

"I think we're safe if we sleep now," Hunter said. "We might wake up insanely early tomorrow, but that will be fine."

Amber increased her pace. Sleep! She had never been so excited to go to bed in her life. When they got back to the room, she quickly undressed and changed to her pajamas. She made a beeline for the bathroom, washing her face, brushing her teeth and using the toilet in record time.

She didn't even wait for Hunter to get ready. She simply slid into the bed, stretched out with a groan, and shut her eyes.

A few minutes later, Hunter kissed her gently. "Good night, I love you."

"I love you," murmured Amber.

She heard Hunter's footsteps on the floor and then her bedroom door close behind him. With that, she drifted into a deep slumber.

Chapter 5

When Amber woke, she glanced over at the clock and saw that it was almost eight o'clock. She stretched and flopped her legs over the side of the bed. Ah! The carpet felt so good between her toes. She found a clean pair of jeans neatly folded in the dresser. Her tee shirts, she was amused to find, were all hanging in the closet. She chose one, slipped it on, and walked over to open the drapes.

Fat rain drops splattered the windows. The sky was darkened by thick clouds. Just as well, Amber thought. She was planning to study her French while Hunter worked from his laptop. She closed the curtains and made her way to the living room.

Hunter was busy typing. Amber waited until he noticed her before planting a kiss on his forehead.

"Have you been up long?"

"About an hour," Hunter said, pausing only to give her a quick smile.

"Sorry, baby. I have to get some things done this morning. There's fresh fruit and bread on the counter. I had an electric tea kettle sent up for you."

"Okay. Thanks."

Amber filled the kettle with fresh water, and plugged it in. She found a selection of teas in a wooden box. Choosing an English Breakfast blend, she soon had a steaming cup by her side when she snuggled up on the sofa and tackled her studies.

At lunch time, Hunter ordered from room service.

"Sorry I can't spend time with you today. You could always take a cab to a museum."

He bit into his turkey and Swiss sandwich.

"No thanks," Amber replied, eyeing one of the pastries that had come with the sandwiches.

She didn't want to admit it, but she was still nervous about going out alone with her limited knowledge of French. Even negotiating a taxi ride seemed daunting.

"I really want to use this time to learn as much French as I can."

"That's my girl," Hunter said. "But remember that as long as you are courteous, most people you would encounter know at least a little English."

"So it's a myth about the rude Parisian?" Amber asked playfully.

"Oh, some of us can be rude," Hunter said, chuckling. "But usually only when provoked. For me it happens when certain people don't take my advice."

Amber laughed. "Some people are just too bossy for their own good."

Later that afternoon, Mrs. Webb called to set up an appointment for the following week. As it would be an informal meeting, she encouraged Amber to dress casually.

It was after six o'clock when Amber finally closed her book for good. She felt as though French phrases were swimming in her head. She was also famished, having only munched on fruit since lunch.

Hunter had gone downstairs to the business center to print out some documents. Amber flipped on the television while she waited, hoping for something mindless to entertain her. Of course everything was in French.

She was in the middle of a show about couples buying houses internationally when Hunter came back, whistling cheerfully.

"Ready for dinner? Still early for Parisians so we won't have to wait long for a table."

"Starving! Are we eating downstairs or out somewhere?"

"Let's go out," Hunter said. "We've been cooped up indoors too much today."

An hour later, they were seated at a casual pizza place filled with students.

"Is this okay?" Hunter asked, raising his voice to be heard above the thump of music in the background.

"Awesome!" Amber said, giving him a thumbs up.

The fancy restaurants were fun in their own way, but it was nice not having to worry about what fork to use. Or drop. Eating with her fingers was an added bonus, she thought, picking up her slice of pizza.

When they returned home, Hunter surprised her by flipping a switch and revealing that the fireplace in the living room worked.

"I thought it was just for show!"

"Sorry. I should have shown you before," Hunter said. "I was afraid it might make you sleepy while you were studying. A nice fire does that to me."

"This is so nice," Amber murmured. "Who needs a television when you can just sit and watch a fire together."

Amber rested her head on Hunter's shoulder. She could stay like this forever.

Chapter 6

The following week, Hunter insisted on taking a break from his internship so that he could accompany Amber to the office.

"After this, I can drop you off every day," he said, waving away her concerns that it lengthened his commute.

"Why would you want to deny me every minute I can be with you?"

"I have a feeling it has more to do with your control freak issues," Amber said, knowing she wasn't going to win this battle.

And she couldn't really argue with spending more time with him. Especially since he would be returning to ridiculous working hours. Hunter had explained that it would be worth the long weekday hours to have the weekends off.

She couldn't argue with that logic. It wasn't ideal, but at least she was here with Hunter instead of pining away alone in the United States.

Amber dressed in black jeans, her new boots, and a soft gray sweater. She had asked Hunter for his opinion, worried about looking too casual.

"Nice choice," he said. "I'm glad we got you the boots. Polishes up the jeans."

He stared for a moment at her arms.

Perplexed, she followed his gaze. Oh! She finally realized that he was searching for the bracelet.

"Still here," she said wryly, pulling it down closer to her wrist. "I never take it off."

Hunter had the grace to blush. As though to apologize, he bent to kiss her.

Amber thought that Hunter was simply going to drop her off at the office building entrance. However, he insisted on following her upstairs and introducing her to the receptionist.

Amber thought the young woman stared a little too long at Hunter. In retaliation, Amber leaned against him protectively. She didn't want any confusion about their relationship.

"Jealous much?"

Hunter led her through the corridors to his mother's office.

Amber ignored him.

"Sweetie! I didn't know you were escorting Amber here!" Mrs. Webb kissed and hugged her son.

"I can't stay." Hunter said before quickly switching to French.

Amber had a suspicion he was talking about her. Of course, she couldn't be certain and didn't want to seem paranoid.

"Of course, Hunter. Don't worry about it."

Mrs. Webb shooed him from the room.

Hunter sent Amber an air kiss and quickly left.

"Now, Amber, let me show you where you'll be working. Then we'll get the tiresome paperwork out of the way. I have so many thoughts to share with you and can't wait to hear your opinions."

Mrs. Webb showed Amber to a large room set up with several small cubicles.

"I'm afraid it isn't fancy, but we've gotten you a new laptop. Oh, and all of our staff are supplied with cell phones." She reached into a drawer and pulled one out.

"Just try to keep it with you at all times. The essential contact numbers have already been entered for you."

Well, that solved Amber's cell phone problem. Her own cheap phone wouldn't work internationally.

"It's great!" Amber said, admiring the office space.

"I love the natural light coming in from the windows. And the view of the city is fabulous."

Mrs. Webb smiled. "Thanks for being so understanding. Hunter told me that you were a simple girl after my own heart."

Amber glowed, pleased that Hunter had talked her up to his mom. An hour later, she was jotting down notes as she spoke with Mrs. Webb.

The Foundation, she quickly learned, was in its infant stage. Mrs. Webb had not been exaggerating when she said that she needed concrete ideas. The two spent a few hours brainstorming how best to develop and run an art program for disadvantaged girls. How old would the students be? Would they apply via a lottery system or was it more fair to look for developing talent in less affluent schools? Should they concentrate on the younger pupils or try to attract high school students who might be able to work toward college scholarships?

A large part of Amber's independent work would be to contact various school districts and universities in the United States. Mrs. Webb was very thorough in her research. She wanted to know what was already being done in this particular field so that she didn't duplicate existing efforts.

Amber suggested aiming the resources at girls taking at least one art course in junior high school in disadvantaged school districts. She explained that many of these girls couldn't afford art supplies beyond pencil and paper. By the time the meeting was over, Amber was excited to be on board. She felt as though she was truly contributing.

Once the introductory meeting was over, Mrs. Webb escorted Amber through the office to introduce her to the rest of the staff.

"You'll just be working for me," she explained. "But I'm sure that everyone will be helpful if you ever need anything."

A major surprise was meeting Kayla's father. Of course, Amber had known that he worked for the company. She had not realized that he had recently been transferred to the Paris office. That explained Kayla's presence here.

However, Mr. Ross was not the type of individual that Amber expected. He was a short, nervous man with a pallid complexion. A swath of oily hair was combed over in a sad attempt at concealing a large, glistening bald spot. His suit was worn and his shoes needed a good polishing. The poor man looked sick and unkempt.

"Mr. Ross is not much of a conversationalist," Mrs. Webb whispered as they moved down the corridor.

"We just transferred him here from the States to head the accounting department. I'm afraid he seems to be having a hard time adjusting."

Finally, the two women circled back to Mrs. Webb's office.

"Hunter told me that he's working late tonight," the elegant woman said. "Please say that you'll have dinner with Mr. Webb and me."

"I don't want to be a burden," Amber murmured, wondering if that was what Hunter was setting up before he left.

"Nonsense, dear! If we can't see Hunter, at least we can share your wonderful company," Mrs. Webb said warmly.

"We're having dinner at home this evening. I've got a simple stew in the crock pot as we speak. Nothing fancy, but we would love to share it with you."

"In that case, count me in. What time should I join you?"

"Why don't you come home with me now? These days I mostly come in just to work with the Foundation."

Mrs. Webb linked her arm in Amber's.

"Let's just grab your coat. I'll have the car meet us downstairs."

As they continued through the corridor, Amber saw Kayla's dad sneaking a glance in her direction. What was it with that family?

Amber had avoided checking her e-mail the last week or so. But now she wondered if there would be further postcard style pictures from Kayla. Perhaps she should check later tonight. There was definitely something weird going on.

All thoughts of Kayla disappeared, though, as Amber slid into the private car with Mrs. Webb. She was offered a drink but only accepted a bottle of water. As Amber chatted with Hunter's mom, the car made its way through packed streets before eventually cruising down a quiet, tree-line avenue of beautiful buildings. As the driver pulled up to the curb, Mrs. Webb explained that they owned one of the apartment buildings.

They had kept the bottom unit for themselves and rented out the other floors. Although the Webbs were clearly wealthy, the personal touches in the home made Amber feel welcome. The walls were covered in paintings. As Mrs. Webb excused herself to check on the stew, Amber wandered around and studied them.

She wasn't surprised to see several art pieces by Hunter. She was startled, though, to discover several more by Mrs. Webb. Had Hunter mentioned that his mother was also an artist? She couldn't remember. She was studying one of the paintings when Mrs. Webb returned with two glasses of wine.

"I know you're not a big drinker, dear. But please pretend to sip so I don't feel embarrassed to have a glass."

Amber giggled. "Just don't give me more than one or I'll be tipsy by dinner."

"I see you've found some of my attempts at painting," Mrs. Webb said. "I wasn't very good, but Mr. Webb insisted that we put them up. I think it reminds him of our early dating days."

Amber smiled. "I didn't realize that you were an artist. I don't think that Hunter ever mentioned it."

"Oh, that was a part of my life before he came along," Mrs. Webb said. "I was one of those aimless students who can't decide what they want to do in life. I flitted from major to major."

"This one is rather good," Amber said. "It radiates a happy feeling."

Mrs. Webb smiled. "My instructor liked that particular one as well. Perhaps it's because I had just fallen in love."

"And then you stopped painting? For good?"

Mrs. Webb shrugged. "Oh, I played around with drawings when Hunter was younger because I wanted to expose him to art at a young age. But I ended up getting a degree in Literature when I graduated."

"Hunter mentioned that you had him a bit late in life?"

Mrs. Webb patted the sofa next to her.

"Please have a seat, dear. And, yes, it seems almost miraculous that we had him at all. I was already in my mid thirties when we married. It took us several years before he was conceived. We had almost given up."

She laughed. "Perhaps that was why he grew up so serious minded. All of our friends had much older children. It wasn't until we moved to the United States that he started hanging around children his own age more regularly."

Amber took a large sip of wine, not sure she should even be asking her next question.

"Has Hunter ever had any negative experience that might make him more protective than the average guy?"

Mrs. Webb smiled wryly. "Beyond you being kidnapped at gun point?"

Amber swallowed. "Uh, yeah. And that was horrible, but he doesn't even want to discuss it."

Mrs. Webb shook her head. "I'm afraid that's more of a guy thing. At least in my experience."

She put her hand on Amber's knee. "When we were trying to conceive, I had three miscarriages."

Amber's hand flew up to her mouth. "Oh, I'm so sorry to hear that."

Mrs. Webb squeezed Amber's hand reassuringly. "It was a long time ago and I've mostly healed from it."

She took a sip of her wine. "The only reason I brought it up is to say that I think that women and men deal with things so differently. Women seem more adept at grieving properly. But men are . . ."

She shrugged her shoulders helplessly.

"My husband was obsessed with pinpointing why each miscarriage happened. He simply wanted to fix things and move on. He didn't want to dwell on the subject."

Amber nodded. "I think that sums up Hunter as well. But he was overly protective even before the kidnapping."

Mrs. Webb pressed her lips together and studied Amber.

"I think it is up to Hunter to share particular parts of his past with you," she said. "All I can say is that you are on the right track."

She held up a warning finger. "But please don't say that I mentioned it to you. He would be devastated that I even hinted about something so private."

Chapter 7

Amber sat there perplexed. So, there was something in Hunter's past, but she wasn't allowed to talk about it. This was even more frustrating than not knowing anything at all!

Mrs. Webb winked.

"Let me show you some photographs, dear," she said, getting to her feet. "I'll be back in a moment."

When she returned, Mrs. Webb was carrying a large box.

"I'm ashamed to say that I've been meaning for years to sort these properly and put them in albums."

"That would be a good job for Hunter," Amber said, grinning.

Mrs. Webb laughed. "You're right, dear. But they would be arranged be in his order. I suppose I'm not willing to relinquish that control to him."

Amber picked a photograph at random and held it up.

"He looks so serious even as a baby!"

Mrs. Webb smiled. "Here's a happier version of him."

She handed over a photograph in which Hunter was laughing, his entire chubby little body exuding joy. In his arms, he clasped a small puppy.

"Hunter loved that dog with a passion," she said and then stood abruptly.

"Perhaps I should check on the stew once more. And I think that I'll make a small salad to go with it."

"Can I help?" Amber asked, standing as well.

The change in Mrs. Webb's manner was so abrupt. Almost as though she was trying to tell her something.

"Oh, no. Please sit and enjoy the photographs."

Amber's head swiveled back to the box. Ah! The answer was here after all. She fingered the picture of Hunter with the puppy. Was that a clue? She set it aside and started to sift through the box.

The photographs were jumbled together in no particular order. High school pictures were mixed in with toddler photographs. An older couple, most likely the grandparents, appeared in many of the images. They apparently lived on a country estate. There were multiple shots of Hunter and the puppy playing on sprawling grounds.

Mrs. Webb returned with a plate of cheese and explained that Mr. Webb would arrive shortly. Amber thanked her and stuffed a bit of cheese in her mouth. But she only found one other photograph that appeared to show a potential calamity with the dog.

Hunter sat by himself in a toy car, his small hands clasping the steering wheel. His brooding gaze was focused just beyond the camera. Although he wasn't crying, he looked melancholy. It was a strange look for such a young child.

Amber checked the time on her phone. Mr. Webb was due to arrive home any minute and she felt guilty for not insisting on helping in the kitchen. She carefully placed all the photographs back into the box. Then she followed the delightful aroma of stew into the kitchen.

Mrs. Webb hummed as she tossed a salad in a rustic, wooden bowl. The kitchen, although equipped with every modern convenience, was in the rustic French style. The long, polished, wooden counter held a lifetime of knife marks and scratches. A simple vase on the table held a large bouquet of ordinary flowers. The effect was warmth plus beauty.

"Can I peek?" Amber asked, pointing to the large crock pot on the counter.

Mrs. Webb smiled and nodded. "I'm going to break down and have an entire bowl if Mr. Webb doesn't arrive soon."

Amber lifted the lid and groaned with pleasure as the wonderful scents hit her nose. The stew bubbled delightfully in the pot. She could see bits of tender beef, carrots, potatoes, beans and corn, all waiting to be tasted.

"I won't tell if you don't," she said, grinning.

"But I might get suspicious if all I get served is salad," a voice said behind her.

Amber jumped. She whirled around and saw Mr. Webb entering the kitchen.

"I didn't mean to startle you, my dear," he said, holding out his arms for a quick hug.

"I'm so pleased that you decided to join us. We were hoping to see more of Hunter with his internship here in Paris."

He shook his head. "I'm afraid he works too much. Not one of the best traits he gets from me."

Mr. Webb turned to his wife, giving her a loving embrace and a kiss on the mouth.

"The stew smells amazing, darling. I'm glad I arrived in time to get some."

Mrs. Webb laughed. "We would have left you a small sample. At least enough to make you hurry home next time."

Amber was dying to ask about Hunter's pet dog, but she realized that Mrs. Webb had already indulged as much as she was comfortable doing so. And if she was honest with herself, she knew that she wouldn't want anyone prying in her personal life behind her back.

Shaking her head, she allowed herself to simply enjoy a pleasant evening with the Webbs. They were so warm and friendly that she quite forgot that they were extraordinarily wealthy. She had expected perhaps servants or the food served on exquisite china. Instead, they ate on large, sturdy plates. The wine glasses, though well crafted, were certainly not fancy crystal. Apparently, Hunter got his simple, everyday tastes from his parents.

After dinner, she was pleasantly surprised to discover Mr. Webb helping his wife with the dishes. Amber was allowed to dry the silverware and plates. Whether they did this every evening or not, it was clear that both of Hunter's parents were quite comfortable in the kitchen. Amber had to admit that it shattered her image of what an insanely wealthy family was like. Apparently, money was simply one small part of the equation.

Finally, Amber looked up and noticed how late it was. The time had passed so quickly. She was wondering how she was going to get back to the hotel when she heard someone walking through the living room. To her delight, Hunter rounded the corner and greeted her with a smile and a kiss.

"Hey, gorgeous! How was your afternoon?"

Amber leaned into him, inhaling his scent. She hadn't realized how much she had been missing him.

"Great!" she said. "I'll fill you in later, but your parents are the most charming hosts ever."

Hunter gave both his parents big hugs and then sniffed the air.

"Mm . . . Mom's famous stew. Is there any left?"

"There's a large bowl with your name on it in the refrigerator," Mrs. Webb replied. "I'll warm it up for you."

"I can get it, Mom. Just let me borrow Amber while it's heating up."

Mr. and Mrs. Webb moved into the living room to give them privacy.

"I trust you had enough to eat," Hunter said, nuzzling Amber's neck with his lips after placing his bowl in the microwave and setting the timer.

"Two bowls of stew, a salad and enough bread to embarrass myself," Amber said with a grin.

She wrapped her arms around him. "Sorry you couldn't join us. Your parents are fun to be around."

Hunter squeezed her in his arms. "I assure you I would have rather been here. The artist I was escorting around the city today was a total jerk."

Amber leaned back and stared at Hunter with surprise.

"He was rude to you?"

Hunter laughed. "Of course not. I would have dropped him off at the nearest metro station. I was supposed to take him to dinner tonight. But after he insulted one of our nicest volunteers, I arranged for dinner to be delivered to his hotel."

"Won't you get in trouble?" Amber asked, dismayed.

Hunter shrugged. "Isabelle understood completely. She doesn't tolerate that behavior toward any of her staff."

He lifted her chin. "But even without her approval, I wasn't going to cater to the whims of that jerk."

Amber smiled. "Any different response would have ruined your reputation."

The microwave dinged and Hunter broke away to get his dish. He grabbed a chunk of leftover bread and dipped it into the juicy stew.

"Ah! This stuff is so good," he said, once he had swallowed his first huge spoonful. "Mom's been making this forever. I think she got the recipe from my grandmother."

Amber was tempted to bring up the puppy, but now was clearly not the time. Instead, she decided on a safer line of questioning that might give her some insights.

"So how far away did your grandparents live from here," she asked innocently, waiting for him to finish chewing to respond.

"About an hour outside of the city," he replied. "I actually stayed there a lot during the summers."

"That must have been fun," Amber said, her voice neutral. "There would be more space for playing in the country side."

Hunter nodded. "Yeah, that was the idea. Give me some fresh air and that sort of thing."

"Did the family sell the property after your grandparents died?"

Hunter gave her a funny look. He looked wary all of a sudden.

"No. Why do you ask?"

"Sorry. I didn't mean to pry," Amber said quickly. "I was just curious. It doesn't matter one way or the other."

Hunter released the tension in his shoulders.

"I forgot for a second who I was talking to," he muttered.

"Hunter Webb! Have you been chatting with other girls?"

Hunter laughed. "Baby, you know you're the only one for me."

He pushed away his empty bowl. "Come over here so I can show you."

Amber put her hands on her hips. She dropped her voice to an indignant whisper.

"There is no way I would ever make out with you in your parent's kitchen. Especially with them in the next room!"

Hunter chuckled, but his eyes were dark.

"If I wanted to, I could prove you wrong," he said, his voice husky.

Amber felt herself melting under the heat of his gaze. His eyes made her tremble.

Hunter smiled slyly.

"Lucky for you, I would never do that to my mother. I simply wanted to give you another hug."

Yeah, right. Like she was going to believe that. Amber stood and carried his dishes to the sink.

"Hunter, do you want to help me wash these up?" she called out loudly over her shoulders.

Hunter started laughing as his mom came in, immediately pushing Amber's hands away from the sink.

"No, darling, leave those. You two should get going so you're not exhausted tomorrow."

Before she knew what was happening, Amber found herself with her coat on and walking out the door after quick hugs from Hunter's parents.

"See you in the morning," Mrs. Webb called as she waved to them from the door.

Hunter ushered her into the car. Oh! Apparently, they were using the car service to get back. Amber noted the new driver. She supposed the drivers operated on a rotating shift if the car was used this much. Unless this was a different car? She had to shove aside the nagging thought that this must cost a fortune.

For the trip back to the hotel, Hunter seemed content to hold her in his arms as she told him about her afternoon at work. She had to give him credit. He sincerely seemed interested in her day.

The only thing on her mind that she couldn't talk about, though, was her suspicion that something terrible had happened to his dog when he was a child. She couldn't simply blurt it out. And why was he sensitive about her question about his grandparent's home?

"Are you okay?" Hunter asked when she grew quiet.

"Just a bit tired," she said, yawning.

"You should go straight to bed when we get home. You're still experiencing a bit of jet lag."

Amber wanted to argue that she would decide if she was ready for bed. But she didn't want such a nice day to end on a sour note. She yawned again. Wow, she was more tired than she imagined.

Hunter shifted behind her and shrugged off his coat. He folded it over and placed it on his lap.

"Lie down and close your eyes, baby," he said softly.

Amber was again too tired to object. Almost as soon as she put her head down, she closed her eyes and drifted to sleep. She vaguely remembered Hunter carrying her through the hotel lobby, taking her boots off and tucking her into bed.

Sometimes having a control freak for a boyfriend wasn't the worst thing in the world.

Chapter 8

Amber was in the break room at the office, refilling her water bottle, when she heard a familiar, unpleasant voice down the hall. Peeking out, she was startled to see Kayla's mother in the middle of an argument with her husband. She darted back into the break room.

Amber knew that the Webbs were out of the office for the next hour or so. Mr. Webb had a meeting with a client and Mrs. Webb had left for a dental appointment. As everyone's schedule got posted on a whiteboard in one of the conference rooms, it would have been easy for Mr. Ross to let his wife know when the Webbs weren't around.

Hmm . . . She was assuming that Mrs. Ross wouldn't visit the office with the Webbs around. She was really getting paranoid now. Then she thought of her name. Mrs. Webb had purposely left it off, afraid that some of the other staff might be tempted to give Amber additional errands in her absence.

"Please know that you are only here to work for me," she told Amber firmly that morning. "I know of a few people who will try to take advantage of having a young person around. But feel free to tell them that is not your responsibility."

Amber smashed her ear against the door.

"Files . . . not working . . . time . . . Amber . . . disaster."

Were they talking about her? Amber strained to hear. The voices started to fade and she peered out the hall cautiously. Mr. and Mrs. Ross walked into an empty conference room.

Amber crept down the hallway, looking for a place to conceal herself. She had to know why they were talking about her.

Along the hall was a storage closet that the cleaners used. Mrs. Webb had pointed it out, explaining that there was an access panel to the women's restroom for plumbers to use in an emergency. Amber slipped inside. The closet door had vertical slats, giving her a clear view of the hallway and the giant copy machine directly opposite of where she stood. Unfortunately, she couldn't hear any conversation from the conference room.

Then she heard the click of heels hitting the tiled corridor. A door whooshed open and someone entered the bathroom. One of the stall doors banged shut. Amber contemplated slipping out and returning to her work area. But then she heard more footsteps in the corridor. Peeking out, she watched Mr. Ross shuffle by, one hand clamped to his forehead as he muttered to himself.

The toilet flushed, startling Amber. She heard water running in the sink and a paper towel being ripped from the dispenser. The whoosh of the opening door was followed by the sharp click of heels. This time, Amber watched Mrs. Ross walk to the copier, one hand on her hip as she tapped her foot impatiently.

A minute later, Mr. Ross reappeared, carrying a thin folder. He handed it to his wife and started to walk away.

But Mrs. Ross restrained her husband.

"Don't be an idiot," she muttered softly. "I'll look suspicious all by myself. Stay here until I'm finished."

"I could have done it after you left," Mr. Ross said, sounding tired and whiny.

"I don't trust you. Last time you left out some of the statements."

"I could get fired for this!" Mr. Ross glanced around uneasily.

Mrs. Ross jabbed her finger at her husband's chest.

"Oh, shut up. If they find out what you've already done, you'll be lucky if that's all they do to you."

Mr. Ross groaned. "I want to stop this. The Webbs are asking if something is wrong at home."

Mrs. Ross grabbed his wrist.

"Tell them you're having health issues. You certainly look ill enough. But I need at least a few more of these for our client."

Amber felt her face flush with anger. What was Mrs. Ross up to? She patted the pockets of her linen slacks. If only she had her cell phone with her. There was no way that anyone was going to believe this without proof.

Mrs. Ross scrutinized the documents as she fed them into the document feeder.

"Wait a second!" she hissed. "This isn't the full report. Half of what I need is missing."

Mr. Ross shrugged helplessly.

"They haven't finished yet. When Hunter left, they postponed the board meeting."

Mrs. Ross slammed the folder down on the copier.

"Why didn't I know this sooner?"

More footsteps sounded in the hallway as another employee passed by on her way to the restroom. Mrs. Ross plastered a fake smile on her face.

"Bonjour, Renee. Comment allez-vous?"

The woman greeted her politely and continued into the restroom.

Mrs. Ross lowered her voice so that Amber could barely hear.

"When I return . . . states . . . better . . . report."

Inside the restroom, the toilet flushed and Mrs. Ross's voice got a bit louder.

"I'll hold the client off as long as I can. But I expect you to provide what I need within three days of that meeting."

"I'll get it for you," Mr. Ross said, his forehead dripping with sweat.

"No. I don't trust you and your ethical issues," Kayla's mother said, making a face.

"Once the board meets, let me know the next time the Webbs are out of the office."

Mrs. Ross stalked away, heading for the lobby. Mr. Ross shuffled back in the direction of his office, looking like a defeated man.

Amber waited several minutes before she crept from the closet. What should she do? Would she look like a paranoid lunatic if she reported what she had overheard? The whole thing sounded ridiculous.

Amber bit her lip. She had to wonder why she was afraid to talk to Hunter about this. Did she really think that he wouldn't believe her? What if something happened and she didn't tell him?

Before she could change her mind, she sent a text.

Amber: Need to talk urgently after you finish work.

Two minutes later, her cell phone rang.

"Amber? Are you okay?" Hunter's voice sounded strained.

"Hunter, I'm fine," she said, "but I need to talk to you tonight."

"I'll be there to pick you up in less than an hour. I'll leave a message for Mom if she isn't back by then."

"Hunter, that's not . . ."

"I'll see you then," Hunter said. The phone went dead.

She hadn't meant to scare him like that.

While she was waiting, she finally opened her private e-mail account out of curiosity. She supposed she was going to have to show him the strange photographs Kayla had e-mailed her as well. She had never even opened the last one because it had come on the morning of her kidnapping.

Amber debated opening it but then decided to wait for Hunter. He was already going to be ticked off that she had kept something from him in the first place. That needed to change, she thought. If she couldn't share everything, then how could they have a strong relationship.

No more than thirty minutes had passed when Amber got a text from Hunter. The car was waiting downstairs, but he insisted on coming up to escort her down.

She was walking down the corridor with her coat when Hunter burst into the front office like a violent storm moving through. His face was stern and his eyes were dark.

Chapter 9

The receptionist gasped as Hunter exploded through the front doors.

He strode up and grabbed Amber, nearly knocking her over in his impatience to get to her. He ran his hands over her face and down her arms, as though expecting that she might have been injured.

For her part, Amber could only gape at him until he seemed satisfied that she was not in some mortal danger. Had he come expecting to find her held hostage again? He was acting as though she might be broken.

Finally, he heaved a sigh of relief and engulfed her in a hug. She felt his heart pounding against her cheek. His whole body trembled in her arms. Okay, he definitely had some issues to work on!

"Hunter, I'm fine. See?" She tried to release herself from his claustrophobic embrace.

Hunter finally let her go and led her out the doors, speaking to the receptionist in such rapid French that Amber, who was still faithfully studying daily, had absolutely no clue what he said. But he waited until she was tucked into the car before he asked her what was going on.

Amber twisted her bracelet nervously.

"I feel like I'm being overly dramatic. Especially the way that you responded. But I overheard something a little while ago and I wasn't sure what to do."

Hunter simply watched her carefully.

"It may or may not be related to something I overheard a while back."

Hunter's beautiful green eyes were flashing like lightning and his lips were in a tight line across his face. The veins in his neck bulged as he struggled to maintain his temper.

"Start at the beginning," he said at last, his voice even and controlled.

For once, Amber didn't hesitate at the order. She related hearing Kayla and her mother plotting in the school building and concluded with recent events at the office.

When she was finished, Hunter wanted more details.

"I'm not clear on how you overheard Kayla and her mother at school."

Amber glared at him.

"I know you're telling the truth. But what are you leaving out?"

"I was sort of behind the candy machine," Amber muttered.

Hunter's eyebrow shot up.

"Why does that not surprise me? I suppose that's how you tore your tee shirt and got the grease stains."

"You noticed?" Amber gaped at him. "Why didn't you ask me about it?"

Hunter glared at her.

"I was trying to practice being less controlling. But it looks like I should have given in to my perfectly normal compulsions!"

"Oh! Well, um . . . I think you did a great job," Amber said lamely. "I had no idea you even noticed the shirt."

Hunter closed his eyes and rubbed a spot in the middle of his forehead. When he spoke again, his voice was resigned.

"I suspect that not even you could manage to hide behind the copier," he said. "So where were you playing detective from today?"

"Um . . . From the cleaning storage closet."

Hunter nodded and, surprisingly, looked impressed.

"Clever. Nobody would ever think to look in there."

"So you're not mad at me?"

Hunter sighed. "I'm angry that you kept things from me. But this new information is helpful."

Amber gaped at him. "You already knew something was going on?"

Hunter frowned. "With Kayla and her mom? No. And that would have been nice to know before now."

Amber twisted in the seat to stare into Hunter's eyes.

"What is going on? And why is my name involved?"

Hunter rubbed his neck.

"Your hunch that Kayla's mom wants to pin something on you is probably right," he mused.

Amber punched his shoulder, shocked that he wasn't more upset.

"How can you say that so calmly? She's obviously doing something illegal!"

But Hunter's temper suddenly flared, and she regretted saying anything at all. His eyes locked onto her like emerald lasers, pinning her to the seat.

"What do I have to do to win your trust?" he asked, his voice almost cold.

Amber folded her arms, her own anger rising.

"Be honest with me! You knew something was going on but said nothing!"

Hunter wasn't backing off.

"Honesty based on your standards? In that case, I have every excuse to wait until things look bad to talk to you."

Amber squirmed under the implication. "But I'm telling you everything now."

"Amber, my dad and I suspected someone in the accounting department was leaking company information. We only recently narrowed it down to Mr. Ross. My mother doesn't even know."

Amber thought back to Mrs. Webb's concerns that Kayla's dad wasn't adjusting well.

"Your dad transferred Mr. Ross here to keep an eye on him?"

Hunter sat back in his seat and folded his own arms across his chest.

"Yes. Obviously, I had no clue that Kayla or her mom were involved or I wouldn't have left you alone when I came here."

"Kayla's dad looks ill." Amber shivered. "The way his wife talks to him is horrible. I kind of feel bad for him."

"Yes, well, he's going to feel a lot worse when I get proof of what they're doing."

Amber thought back to the conversation she had overheard.

"So what's so important about this Board Meeting coming up?"

Hunter looked pained. "I'm sorry, but I can't talk about it with you."

Amber glared at him. "So who has trust issues now?"

"Honestly, Amber, it's not like that. The only people who know are on the Board. That's twelve people, including me and my parents."

Hunter shook his head. "I don't want this work situation to come between us. I promise I'm telling you all that I can without compromising my responsibility to the company."

Amber softened. "I don't want to fight anymore."

"Me either, baby. Especially if it's not the kind of fight that would lead to some passionate kissing." Hunter grinned slyly.

Amber stared at Hunter, seeing the person she loved. She remembered that horrible time when she thought she might die. Why was she letting this situation pull them apart?

Chapter 10

Later that evening, Hunter took her to an intimate restaurant and she happily dug into each course set before her.

"That's quite an appetite you've got there," Hunter said, smirking.

"You aren't exactly leaving your food untouched," Amber pointed out, laughing.

By the time the main course came, however, Amber had to slow down.

As she was slowly chewing a bite of rare steak, she noticed that Hunter was uncharacteristically quiet.

"Everything okay?"

"I was just thinking," Hunter said hesitantly. "I was rude the other day when you asked about my grandparent's property."

Amber waved her fork. "Don't worry about it."

Hunter ignored her. "The thing is that I haven't been back since my grandmother passed away."

Amber put her fork down, shocked that Hunter was opening up to her. She noticed that he was pushing his food around in a big circle on his plate. This was clearly difficult for him to talk about.

"And there was . . ."

Suddenly Hunter stopped and stiffened. It was as though he had hit a limit. He tried to cover his nerves by taking a large swallow of wine.

"So, anyway," he said, refocusing, "I just didn't want you to think I was upset by anything you said."

Hunter had been making a mountain out of his mashed potatoes and suddenly realized what he was doing. He flattened it with one firm slap of his fork.

"I'm not like you," he said, staring at her with admiration. "You face up to your fears without any hesitation. I'm more of a wimp."

Amber took his hand. "It's okay to face things with baby steps."

Hunter laughed bitterly. "That's what the therapists used to tell me."

Therapists?

"Are you seeing anyone now?" Amber asked, suddenly alarmed she hadn't known.

"No, that was back when I was a kid. But I was stubborn and mom finally gave up taking me."

"No!" Amber clutched her heart in mock surprise.

Hunter laughed. "I was convinced that they didn't know what they were talking about. I sat in their offices and won our staring contests."

He smiled wryly. "And see what a wonderful person I turned out to be."

Amber squeezed his hand.

"You are a great guy, Hunter Webb. I'll help you face any ghosts in your past."

"I almost feel sorry for them," Hunter said, his eyes twinkling. "You can be pretty scary when you're angry."

"Just don't forget it."

She shoved his fork aside with her own and scooped up a bite of his potatoes.

"It's such a shame to waste food. I'm not too ashamed to pillage from your plate in a five star restaurant."

Hunter tried not to smile. "Go ahead. I won't report you."

Amber hesitated until she noticed the elderly woman glaring at her from the next table. Really? Amber smiled sweetly at the woman, turned her head and flagrantly ate several bites from Hunter's plate.

More than irritating the snoopy old lady, Amber knew that Hunter needed the diversion. He seemed almost fragile this evening. She watched with a satisfied smile as Hunter held his napkin over his mouth to hide his laughter.

The offended woman began speaking in rapid French to her husband. But the husband, a kindly looking gentleman with snow white hair, merely smiled charmingly in Amber's direction.

Hunter was still chuckling when they got back into the car to return to the hotel.

"That poor guy is probably sleeping on the sofa tonight for showing you sympathy."

Amber smiled. "She shouldn't have looked at me like I was a naughty child. It made me want to prove her right."

Today had been such an emotional roller coaster day and she was starting to feel its effects.

Hunter was quiet as they arrived at the hotel and took the elevator back up to their room.

Amber didn't want to interrupt his thoughts. But she couldn't put off the question that had been on her mind most of the evening.

"So where do we go from here? I mean, with the whole Ross family situation."

"That depends," Hunter said, with a hint of a smile. "Do you want to help catch a thief?"

"You'll let me help? Are you feverish?" She reached up and touched his forehead with mock alarm.

Hunter regarded her sternly. "Only if you follow every single direction I give you. No questions asked."

"Yes! Yes!" Amber agreed.

"I'm serious, Amber. I don't want you in any situation that could get out of control."

"Fine. Hunter, I'm so proud of you!"

Hunter grimaced. "Why am I already regretting this?"

Amber kissed him.

Chapter 11

Hunter strode into his family's company office as though he owned the place. Well, he did in fact own a third of the company. Sometimes he wondered why the company still gave him a thrill. His real passion, painting, captivated him much more than the board room. Still, he enjoyed working on special projects with his father every now and then.

Perhaps some of his feeling came from a sense of obligation. He knew that every advantage he had in life came directly as the result of both his parents and his deceased grandparents building up the company.

Still, his parents had always kept him grounded, forever teaching by example that one could have a life of luxury while still practicing a certain humbleness. He wasn't sure how many other rich kids had grown up learning to clean toilets, scrub the shower, do laundry, and cook their own food. While he no longer cleaned the toilets, he appreciated his mother's insistence on him being grounded.

"Bonjour, Monsieur Webb." The perky receptionist batted her lashes at him.

He smiled at the thin, blonde woman who was trying to flirt with him. Although he found her attention flattering, he was mostly amused to think about how Amber would react if she was watching.

"Bonjour, Juliette," he replied pleasantly. "Has Monsieur Ross arrived?"

"No, Monsieur Webb. Shall I call you when he does?"

The receptionist shifted so that her cleavage was a bit more noticeable.

"That won't be necessary, Juliette. In fact, I do not wish to be disturbed. I would appreciate it if no one, including Monsieur Ross, knows that I am even in the office today."

"Certainly, Monsieur Webb. I'll make sure that no calls are forwarded to your office."

"Thank you, Juliette. That would be wonderful."

Hunter took one quick look behind him when he heard the elevator ding and hurried through the office. As he turned the corner, he heard Kayla Ross question the receptionist.

"But I'm sure I just saw him," he heard Kayla say.

"I'm sorry, Mademoiselle Ross. Monsieur Webb is not in the office today."

Hunter didn't stay to hear the rest. He quickly approached his hiding spot. He hadn't expected Kayla to show up, but maybe it was for the best. Now he could see if she was a pawn for her mother or part of the conspiracy to steal company secrets through her father.

Hunter still couldn't believe that he was using Amber's hiding place. She was really something else. She drove him insane at times with her reckless behavior. But in spite of that, he was madly in love with her. For the first time in his life, he had found somebody who didn't appear to be after his money. If anything, she could be a pain about accepting the luxuries he was forever trying to give her.

He smiled, thinking of how her eyes blazed when she was angry. He even loved her fiery temper.

Hunter slipped into the supply closet across the hall from the photocopier. As his eyes grew adjusted to the dimness, he saw the corner where the cleaning staff kept mops, buckets and cleaners. Most of the staff didn't know that the closet also led directly to the women's restroom. Apparently, it enabled plumbers to reach certain pipes in an emergency.

Hunter pictured Amber lurking in the closet as she eavesdropped on the Ross family. Only Amber would have placed herself in that situation. He shook his head.

Hunter's palms grew sweaty as he thought about how he had finally confided to his parents that he planned to ask Amber to marry him. To be honest, he was afraid that she might not say yes. Even though she had assured him that she loved him, he knew that she found his controlling tendencies to be unacceptable.

But Hunter did not want to give her up. From the very first time he held her (passed out from hunger), he had felt an electricity between them. And that was even before he kissed her for the first time.

Hunter's musings were interrupted by the sound of heels clicking in the corridor. He heard whispers and strained to hear. He couldn't see much from the slats of the closet door. Fortunately, he and the security guard had ascertained that nobody could see in the darkened closet. Realistically, he didn't even need to be here. But he wanted to be a first witness to what was happening.

He smiled. Yes, he was that controlling. There was no way he was going to stay away even knowing that the security team had set up hidden cameras and microphones over the weekend.

Mrs. Ross didn't even work at the company. But her weak-willed husband worked in accounting. Hunter's Dad had first suspected that somebody was embezzling from the home office in the United States. When the search narrowed down to Mr. Ross, Hunter and his father devised a plan to trap the man. They gave him a promotion so that he was forced to work here in Paris.

Over the last few months Mr. Ross started acting suspiciously, growing fidgety around Hunter, his father, and the other employees. He was never a particularly well dressed man, but now he often came to work in crumpled clothing. In addition to that, he appeared to have lost weight and he looked ill. Hunter's mom, not knowing what was going on, had asked if perhaps the man needed medical attention.

Hunter knew that his Dad normally didn't keep anything from his wife. But Hunter's mom would have never done well as a poker player or a spy. She simply could not keep secrets. Even when she attempted to, her face often gave her away. Hunter had not planned on telling Amber either, but she stumbled onto everything the week before.

Hunter frowned as he adjusted his mini digital recorder. He was trying to give Amber more space, even allowing her to participate today when he would rather have seen her safe at home. He tried not to think about the murderous look in her eyes when he told her that she was in charge of the "get away" car.

Any marriage proposal was going to have to wait until she cooled off. She was definitely going to be angry at him for several days. Was he being too controlling? He didn't think so. But why did he feel so guilty at the moment?

But he had a right to be concerned! It had only been mere weeks since she had been held at gunpoint, kidnapped, and left to freeze to death on abandoned property. And, yes, he had been a control freak and had given her a bracelet with a tracking chip. But that bracelet had been the only way that the police had been able to track her and save her life.

Hunter suddenly tensed as he realized that footsteps had stopped near the accounting offices. Lifting the mini recorder to his eye, he poked a special lens through the slats and waited.

He couldn't hear anything for several minutes. Then he heard a door shut and heels clicking down the corridor once more. He pressed the record button. A moment later, both Mrs. Ross and her daughter Kayla paused at the photocopier.

"Let's get this done quickly. I don't know why your father is stalling on that last report. I'm beginning to think that he's chickening out."

"I wonder why," Kayla said, her voice low but angry. "Dad looks terrible. This whole thing is giving him a nervous breakdown."

When Mrs. Ross responded, her voice was cold and uncaring.

"If he does what I tell him to do, he earns a nice vacation on a faraway beach. And when I divorce him, I'll even be nice and let him keep a little bit to live on."

"Aren't you the generous one?" Kayla asked, her voice cold.

"Don't use that tone with me, young lady, or you can live with your father when this is all over. Now make yourself useful and start copying these things."

"I don't know how to use this thing. I'm not some low life secretary," Kayla replied.

Hunter watched as Mrs. Ross stiffened. He knew from his mother that the woman had grown up in a blue collar family. Mrs. Ross had worked as a secretary until she met her husband. Although Hunter knew that Kayla could vicious, he had never realized that she had gotten her attitude directly from her mother.

He didn't want to be sympathetic to Kayla. She had pursued him relentlessly for years in spite of his constant rejections. Worse, she had insinuated that he was dating her at the beginning of his relationship with Amber. Thankfully, Amber was a strong girl in her own right and had stood up to her. But that didn't make him like Kayla any better. Still, he couldn't imagine growing up with a cold mother like Mrs. Ross.

That was another thing he loved about Amber. In spite of a bad childhood, she was one of the most generous and loving people he knew. He was convinced she didn't have a selfish bone in her body. Another reason to want to make her his wife. Beautiful, kind, and smart. She was also a talented artist who understood the primal feelings that art created in him.

"Watch your mouth, young lady. Or you won't see a penny of inheritance."

"The way you plow through money, there won't be any left anyway," Kayla muttered.

"What was that, young lady?"

"Nothing," Kayla said darkly. "How many copies do you need of this?"

Hunter had trouble concentrating on their irritating chatter. This might be his hardest task of the whole day.

He was so absorbed keeping the recorder steady that he was startled by a sound in the corner of the closet. He jerked his head around and realized that somebody was in the restroom. Worse, they were trying to open the mesh screen that led inside the closet. He flattened himself against the back of the closet.

Who would be on the other end?

Chapter 12

Amber fumed as she sat in the luxurious Towne Car, feeling ridiculous in her tight black leggings, black boots, and snug black turtleneck. A secret spy with no place to go.

She couldn't believe that she had taken Hunter's assurances that she would be part of his plot to catch the couple stealing secrets from his family's company. She grimaced as she realized how easily he had fooled her. Now, here she was stuck in the so-called "getaway car" waiting for him to complete the whole operation entirely on his own.

Frustrated, she leaned back in her seat and peeked into the min fridge. This was worse than not being involved at all, she thought irritably as she popped the tab on a diet soda. Then again, she probably should have expected something this low from Hunter. He couldn't seem to resist treating her like a child. Insisting that she stay in the car like some toddler!

She was just as angry with herself, though. Why hadn't she simply told Hunter how she felt and insisted on coming along? She sighed, rubbing her forehead. Well, didn't she already know the answer to that? As ridiculous as it seemed, she was certain that Hunter wasn't bluffing when he said he would call the whole thing off if it meant a risk to her personal safety.

Okay, for the ordinary woman, maybe that was a good thing. But Hunter had such control issues that it drove her bananas. Yes, he had saved her life just a month earlier. She wasn't discounting that. Or was she?

Amber pounded her fists on the back of the seat. She just wanted to be herself! Yes, she obviously got herself into some bad situations. But what would life be like living as though she was a fragile flower. She didn't want to be an orchid in a beautiful vase.

With that thought, Amber remembered that she was not in the car by herself. She saw the driver's eyes in the mirror and felt her face flushing. Great! She must seem like a three-year-old throwing a temper tantrum. The driver grinned at her and then quickly averted his eyes.

Amber pretended to be preoccupied with the view outside her window. The car was parked across the street from the office building. Had she turned a moment sooner or a moment later, she might have missed what happened next. First, one cab pulled up front and Kayla Ross stepped out. Another cab pulled up soon after and Mrs. Ross got out. She walked inside the building just minutes after her daughter.

Amber grabbed her large briefcase. This was so not fair! Hunter had no right to order her around. Today was the perfect opportunity to show him that she could take care of herself and help out.

Decision made, Amber found herself grinning.

Her conscience attempted to change her mind.

This is a terrible idea. Hunter is going to be livid.

Amber ignored the ominous warning.

Opening the briefcase, Amber whipped out a gorgeous red wig and a wraparound skirt that was as thin and airy as a filmy scarf. She even had a matching neck scarf to go with it. Very fashionable! She had secretly practiced putting the wig on the day before. Now she was comfortable with only a quick glance in her compact mirror to make sure that it fit properly.

"Sorry in advance for any yelling you might hear from Hunter," she told the driver, giving him a grin.

To her surprise, the driver merely winked like a conspirator before quickly exiting the car and getting the door for her.

"I don't know anything about anything," he said, shrugging. "I just sit in the car until I'm told the next desired destination."

"Thanks!" Amber climbed out of the car.

"Good luck!" the driver called out after her.

Amber grinned and hurried across the street, taking advantage of a momentary loll in traffic. Only two drivers screamed and blared their horns at her.

She slowed and caught her breath as she entered the building. Although one of the guards gave her an appraising look, he clearly did not recognize her. Good!

She took the elevator to one floor below her destination. Even if no one recognized her, other employees would want to know what she was doing there if she waltzed through the front door.

Once in the elevator, she stared at herself in the mirror. With the wig and fake glasses, she looked like a completely different person. Maybe she should consider dying her hair the same lovely shade of red as the wig. She felt more confident in her disguise.

The elevator dinged and the doors swung open. Two businessmen waited to enter. She smiled at them brightly. One smiled flirtatiously with her. Focus, Amber, she told herself as she walked casually toward an office. But as soon as the elevator doors shut, she hurried to a gray door in the corner.

The stairwell had a musty smell to it. Amber grimaced as she started up several flights of stairs. Good thing she had not had to walk up the entire thing as the company took up the top floor.

Of course, Amber had fantasized that she would be at Hunter's side while they played a high game stakes of spying. That is, until Hunter had swiftly vetoed that idea. Amber bit her lip. She still wasn't sure exactly what she was going to do.

At the top of the stairwell, she hesitated a moment, her palms sweaty. The door had a keypad for entry. This wasn't a hindrance since she had the code. She just hoped that nobody was walking by the door. A strange redhead would attract attention.

Amber quickly tapped in the appropriate code, reached up to adjust her fake glasses, and then gently twisted the handle. She pushed the door open wide enough to glimpse inside. She pressed her ear to the edge of the opening. When she heard nothing, she swung the door open all the way and strode inside. Success! She fought an impulse to pump her fist.

Okay, now she had to get to that supply closet without attracting attention. She was almost there when she heard footsteps in the hall. She wheeled and darted into the restroom. Her boot heels clicking, she hurried to the stall. She had just slammed the door shut when she heard the swoosh of the restroom door opening. Just in time! She peeked out the crack between the stall door and wall and saw Kayla primping at the mirror.

Kayla placed a purse on the counter and began to rummage for makeup supplies. She could be there for a while.

Amber felt sweat pool beneath her armpits. She started to doubt herself. What was Hunter going to do when she showed up?

Her annoying conscience had a response for that.

He's going to go control freak crazy. Again, this is a bad idea.

Without even thinking, Amber groaned out loud in frustration.

Kayla froze, then looked disgusted.

Amber realized that the girl must think that she had diarrhea. She smirked. From experience, she knew that if she was in Kayla's position, she would be leaving very quickly to avoid any unpleasant odors. Grinning, Amber moaned again and started pawing at the tissue roller, noisily gathering up handfuls of tissue.

Kayla grimaced and quickly stuffed her lipstick and powder compact back into her purse. She nearly ran from the restroom, her heels clicking noisily on the tiled floor.

Chapter 13

Amber smiled and exited the stall. She headed straight for a large vent in the corner of the room. Hunter's mom had told her that this particular vent led directly into the maintenance closet to allow plumbers access to the pipes. Reaching into her purse, she pulled out a small screwdriver and quickly removed several small screws holding the thick mesh screen in place. She removed it, set it to one side and peeked in.

The room was dimly lit but she didn't see Hunter. Hmm. That was strange. He definitely had time to get here already. Or had he only told her part of his plan? Was he planning to do more than simply hang out in the storage closet and film the Ross family as they tried to photocopy classified documents?

Hearing footsteps in the hall once more, she moved inside the maintenance closet and quickly held up the mesh screen. Hopefully, nobody could see that it had been tampered with. As the footsteps continued down the hallway, she gently propped the screen in place the best she could. She stepped around a metal buck on wheels, moving to peek out the slats of the closet door.

But before she could move any further, a hand reached around and covered her mouth.

Amber felt her heart lurch in her chest. She tried to scream but the hand only tightened against her mouth. And then she heard a familiar whisper.

"Be quiet!" Hunter warned and Amber nodded numbly, realizing that he hadn't recognized her yet.

This could get ugly, she thought, her heart still beating so hard that her chest hurt. Or maybe that was just the tension from being grabbed like that.

She turned around and saw the recognition slowly start to appear in Hunter's eyes. First, there was a glimmer of confusion. Then those beautiful green eyes, still sparkling in the dimness of the closet, darkened as he realized what she had done.

His mouth twitched and Amber saw the veins jump in his neck. Yeah, he was close to freaking out on her. But before he could say a word, heels clicked down the hallway and they both jumped.

Amber wanted to say something, anything, to make things right. She tried to get close enough to whisper to him. But he was focused on the slats of the door and only held up a hand in warning for her to remain quiet.

Amber suddenly wondered if they were walking into a trap. What if either Kayla or her parents had seen Hunter enter the building? All too late, she remembered that a security camera showed everyone entering the building. No one would recognize her with the red wig, but Hunter would be easy to spot.

Amber put a hand on Hunter's arm and pointed to the screen. She mimed leaving. But Hunter only pointed his finger at her and nodded a firm agreement that she was to leave. Amber tried once again to move close enough to whisper but Hunter stubbornly ignored her.

Feeling an ominous tension, Amber slid back. Her boot caught the edge of the metal bucket. It turned over with a loud clank.

Outside the closet, there was a startled yelp.

Amber stopped, horrified. But Hunter angrily motioned her toward the mesh screen.

"I swear I heard something in the closet!"

Amber froze. If this thing went south, it would be all her fault.

"I heard something too," Mrs. Ross muttered.

Fear made Amber move quickly. She slipped through the gap in the wall.

Hunter was right behind her and replaced the screen in one fluid motion. He pointed to the slots where the screws went and Amber's hands flew to her purse.

"We know you're in there. You might as well come out," Mrs. Ross said in a low voice.

Amber was shaking so hard that Hunter took the purse from her. He yanked out the plastic bag holding the screws and screwdriver. He quickly started putting them back in.

"Kayla, open the door slowly and then stand back," Mrs. Ross ordered.

"Me? Why don't you open it?"

Amber finally got her nerves back and helped Hunter. How were they supposed to get out of the restroom without anyone seeing them? This was all her fault.

The only thing helping now was that Mrs. Ross and Kayla were arguing softly. Their voices buzzed in the corridor.

Amber couldn't even blame Hunter for getting angry. She was quite furious at herself. And she wanted to do something that would fix things. If only they had a diversion while Kayla and her mom were focused on the closet door.

Rummaging in her purse, she felt something cold and metal in the bottom. She pulled it out, not even sure when she had put a wine bottle opener in there. But it was about the perfect size.

Hunter stared at her for a second. But he must have figured out what she was thinking because he nodded quickly, took the opener from her, and moved toward the door.

Amber held her breath as Hunter quietly pulled the door open and tensed with his arm raised, the wine opener clenched in his fist.

He looked back, as though to make sure that she understood that they were going to have to move fast. Then he looked down at her feet, nodded, and removed his shoes.

Oh! Good idea. Stomping down the hallway in her boots was not ideal for a furtive escape. She had just slipped off the second boot when more footsteps clattered down the hallway. Heels. Definitely a woman.

Hunter closed the door and hurried over to a stall.

Amber quickly followed, hoping that the woman was not going to the restroom. No such luck. Mere seconds later, the door swooshed open.

Amber's heart thumped painfully as she squatted on top of the toilet, her stockinged feet gripping the smooth seat. One wrong move and she would have a soggy foot. But she couldn't risk the bizarre appearance of bare stockinged feet if anyone glanced under the stall door. Even though she had locked the stall door, her hands were sweaty as she pressed her palms against the sides of the stall walls for balance. She could only hope that Hunter was similarly hidden.

Fortunately, it was a large restroom and the woman walked past the stalls where they were hidden, her heels clicking loudly on the tiled floor. Amber wondered fearfully if Kayla or Mrs. Ross would figure out the link between the closet and the restroom. Time seemed to slow. Finally, the woman finished her business and left.

Amber crept off the toilet seat, and eased out of the stall. Hunter was already by the door, impatiently waiting for her. She slipped behind him and waited, listening as the woman's heel clicks grew softer as she moved further down the hallway.

"She's gone," Kayla whispered just a few feet outside the door from them.

Using her compact mirror, Amber could see that Kayla and Mrs. Ross were huddled by the copier as though discussing business.

Beside her, Hunter didn't hesitate. His arm swung up while the two women were still looking away. The wine opener sailed from his hand and pinged against an air-conditioning vent far down the hall.

Predictably, Kayla and her mother started down the hallway to investigate. The two women didn't bother being quiet so it was even easier to slip out of the restroom without being heard. Racing on bare feet, Amber followed Hunter down the hall and around the corner. Thank goodness that the stairwell door was in this direction.

A few minutes later, both she and Hunter were safely in the stairwell. Amber wanted to sit down and let her nerves settle. But Hunter was already slipping his shoes back on. She started thinking about how ridiculous this whole event was. What must Hunter feel like slinking around his family's company office as though he was the one with something to hide?

Without speaking, Amber silently slid her own boots back on. She felt sick thinking about how she had nearly blown the whole thing for Hunter. That wasn't going to be easy to live down, especially since she had willfully disobeyed him. In fact, she was a little surprised that he hadn't already said something. Except, of course, that Kayla and her mom were still in the building and now completely free to continue their illegal activities.

Amber felt pretty low as she followed Hunter down the stairs. They had to walk the whole way down because each floor's interior doors had security locks keyed for each individual company.

Amber was breathing hard but wasn't about to complain when they finally reached the bottom. She was also prepared to have to wait it out by herself in the lobby. She had a feeling that Hunter would be headed right back up to the office.

To her surprise, Hunter gripped her elbow and headed straight for the elevator. There were other passengers coming out, but she and Hunter were the only ones headed up.

When Hunter started speaking, Amber meekly listened.

"I had a feeling that you weren't going to listen to me," he said, softer than she expected.

This sensitive side had an unnerving effect on Amber. She would have preferred that Hunter had gotten angry. This sounded like . . . well, like he had expected to be disappointed in her. That hurt more.

The truth was that she had simply wanted to be part of the action. She had charged into the building with no clearly defined plan. Why else had she put the wig and skirt wrap in her briefcase that morning? Hadn't she avoided showing Hunter the wig this weekend? Hadn't she sneaked it into the hotel room? She had merely been looking for an excuse, any excuse, to intervene.

"I'm sorry," she said, just as softly.

Once again, Hunter surprised her by simply shaking his head.

"I am too, but we'll talk about it later."

Reaching into the inside pocket of his suit jacket, he pulled out a small video camera.

"But now you're part of this and I need you."

Amber brightened considerably, but she tried to keep her level of rising excitement hidden. He was going to let her help! Okay, so maybe she had interfered to the point where he had no choice. But, still.

"There are already cameras and microphones in the hallway by the copier. Also in the area where Mr. Ross works. But just in case, I want you to go to the back conference room. They'll be too antsy to talk openly in the hallway now."

Right, Amber thought. Because I'm the one that spooked them by making a racket in the closet.

"Keep the wig and those fake glasses on just to be on the safe side. When we go in the front door, I'll say that you are a new client and that we'll be using the back conference room. Then, I'll walk you in right in front of Kayla and Mrs. Ross."

"What are you going to do?"

Hunter kept talking as though he hadn't heard her.

"You'll stay in the conference room," he said, giving her a hard look.

"Yes," she said, reacting as though his words were stinging whips.

"The camera is small enough you can stick one end in your purse. Use your scarf to drape over the top and nobody should notice it. But I'm hoping that you'll be in there alone. This is only on the chance that they come in there to talk."

"What if they ask me to leave?"

"If they even start to come in, you leave immediately and say that you are headed to the restroom. That way, you can leave your purse on the table and not look suspicious."

"Right. Sounds good," Amber said, suddenly not able to look at him.

Unexpectedly, Hunter leaned down, tilted her chin back and gave her a kiss on the mouth.

"I still love you," he said softly. "Even though you've made my blood boil today by your reckless behavior."

"I love you too," Amber said. "Be careful."

Seconds later, the elevator stopped and Hunter pulled her out quickly, tugging on her hand.

Amber reached her free hand up to make sure that her wig was securely in place just before Hunter swooped into the front lobby with her.

Hunter fired off a rapid greeting to the receptionist, nodded briefly in Amber's direction, and then continued on through the office without even breaking his stride. Amber had to jog to keep up with him, but she understood his urgency.

Perhaps Hunter had planned on whisking her to the conference room without an encounter with anyone in the Ross family. But Kayla and her mother were both in the hallway. This time, however, they were busy feeding bundles of documents into the photocopier.

As Amber and Hunter strode down the hallway, Kayla's eyes got huge. But Mrs. Ross narrowed her eyes as though she was simply irritated that she had been caught.

"Hello, Kayla. Mrs. Ross. What a surprise to meet you like this."

Chapter 14

"I told you that I saw him earlier!" Kayla said triumphantly. "And you didn't believe me!"

"So what exactly are you doing here, Hunter?" Mrs. Ross asked, her voice as cold and hard as a slab of marble.

Amber stared ahead, trying not to give herself away. She couldn't look at Hunter, but she could almost picture his eyebrows shooting up at the question.

"Unlike either of you, I own part of this company. That kind of gives me the right to be here any time I wish."

Hunter's voice was deadly calm.

Mrs. Ross tried another tactic. A forced smile stretched across her face.

"Sorry, Hunter. You startled us. Our printer at home is on the blink and I decided to stop by and photocopy a few things. I hope it's okay."

Hunter returned her fake smile.

"I wish I had known. I would have had my new assistant take care of it for you."

Hunter moved to the machine.

"Jessica, why don't you finish this job for my dear friends."

It took Amber a second to realize that she was supposed to be Jessica.

"Oh, that won't be necessary," Mrs. Ross said, blocking Hunter with her body.

"I'm sure that your assistant has more important things to do than to take care of my personal documents."

"Interestingly enough, she has extra time on her hands today. I was hoping to find something for her to do."

Amber peeked at Hunter's face. Though he continued to smile, his eyes showed his fury. Those gorgeous green eyes were stormy as the sea. She was glad she wasn't on the receiving end of that look.

Mrs. Ross laughed. "You're being such a sweet gentleman. But I really must insist on finishing this ourselves. We have some sensitive tax information."

"Oh, dear me! Then I prefer you not use the photocopier. I'm afraid of the liability if something sensitive goes missing."

Mrs. Ross tried to maintain her smile. "I'm sure that your mother would want you to treat me a bit more respectfully."

Hunter's face scrunched in concern.

"My dear Mrs. Ross. How have I offended you? I simply want to keep your confidential papers secure."

"I can take responsibility for my papers. Surely you have other important matters to attend to than babysitting me while I try to get a few things copied."

"I have all day, Mrs. Ross!" Hunter exclaimed. "Can you believe it? I wasn't even supposed to be in today. But my schedule unexpectedly changed."

He held out an arm. "Come on. Let me take you to the conference room and get you a cup of coffee. I haven't seen you in awhile and I'd love to catch up."

At just that moment, a few employees walked by. Mrs. Ross eyed them warily and then decided it would look suspicious so leave Hunter there with his hand extended in front of him.

"Kayla, finish up this set and wait for your father to bring the rest," she said, with a hard look at her daughter.

Hunter turned and smiled at Amber.

"Jessica, be a dear and give Kayla a hand with the papers."

"Um . . . Yes, Sir," Amber responded in a high voice.

She was going for a French accent but saw Hunter roll his eyes. Hopefully, Kayla and Mrs. Ross wouldn't hear the false notes. But then she remembered the camera that Hunter had already slipped into her purse.

"Excuse me, Mr. Webb!" she called out nervously. "Could you just take my purse and put it down somewhere for me?"

Hunter's hand moved to the front of his jacket before he stopped short.

"Let me just get out my wallet," Amber said lamely, making sure her fingers covered both the wallet and the camera.

Hunter stepped up, blocking her hand from view of either Kayla or her mother. Amber quickly stuck the camera in his hand.

"Oh, silly me! I forgot I have no pockets in this dress," she announced.

Hunter turned so that both women could see her stuff the wallet back into the purse.

Amber's cheeks burned from her terrible job as an actress. But at least Hunter now had the camera in hand.

"Jessica, why don't you check the paper supply?" Hunter asked in a casual, almost bored voice.

"I heard the receptionist grumbling that we were low on paper when I came in."

Amber blinked and nodded.

"Yes, Sir!"

Was that a hidden message? She obediently opened the closet and pulled out a ream of paper. At least this would buy a little time.

"Let me just fill this up first," she said to Kayla, blocking the girl from feeding more documents through.

She knelt with the ream of paper. "If it gets too low, the whole thing jams up and starts chewing up the original documents."

"I'm sure it's fine," Kayla said, trying to move her away.

"Oh, but I'll be blamed if anything happens to your papers."

Kayla sighed as she stepped back. "Please hurry! My mother is not the most patient person in the world."

Amber pulled out several of the trays.

"Oh, dear, Mademoiselle. This doesn't look good. I think something is already stuck in this back mechanism here. Give me a second to get it out."

Reaching deep into the machine, Amber pretended to tug at something.

"Don't tear it!" Kayla pleaded, suddenly alarmed.

Amber pretended to use both hands. She subtly crumpled the end of a paper and jerked upward, making sure that the paper tore as she stumbled backwards. She reached behind herself, as though to prevent herself from falling, and shoved the folder of papers onto the floor.

"Oh, my goodness, Mademoiselle," she said shrilly, bending as though to recover the papers scattered on the floor. Instead, she shoved them further out, making an even worse mess of things.

"You clumsy idiot!" Kayla shrieked, dropping to the floor and scrambling in all directions.

Amber grabbed as many papers as she could while wailing loudly.

"Oh, I am so terribly sorry, Mademoiselle! Oh, please don't tell my new boss! Oh, I can't lose another job. My bills are due!"

Meanwhile, Amber thrashed across the floor, knocking into Kayla every time the girl succeeded in getting an armful of papers.

Employees poured out of their offices to see what the commotion was. Even Mr. Ross showed up. But, strangely enough, Amber didn't see Hunter or Mrs. Ross. There was no way that either hadn't heard the chaos.

"Oh, what is this?" Amber cried, seeing one of the officers of the company step into the hall.

"These are company files!" Amber innocently turned to Kayla. "Mademoiselle, you are in possession of our company's very sensitive files!"

Kayla looked panicked as she stood up, looking around furtively. She started to back away, but a security officer put an arm on her shoulder.

"I'd like to speak with you, young lady," he said, motioning to another security guard to join him as he advanced in Kayla's direction.

"And who are you?" he asked, looking pointedly at Amber.

"She's with me. Don't worry about her."

Amber jumped as she felt Hunter's arm touch her waist.

"We can go now," he whispered in her ear. "Our security guys have all they need. My dad is already waiting for the police to arrive. I'll give them my statement later."

Amber followed Hunter out through a throng of curious employees. When they got to the reception area, Mrs. Ross was screaming at a police officer.

"You can't keep me here. I was just visiting my husband. I'll sue this company for harassment!"

Hunter ignored the commotion and headed for the door. With a nod of his head, both he and Amber were allowed to leave.

"You might want to take this before someone thinks I just robbed you," Hunter said as they stood by the elevators.

Amber noticed her purse in his hand for the first time. She suddenly felt as weak and spent as though she had run a couple of miles.

"Are you okay?" Hunter slid an arm around her waist.

"That was a little tense in there," Amber said, wanting to simply snuggle up against his body and forget all that had just happened. Her nerves were on edge.

"Nobody was in any actual danger," Hunter said, squeezing her against his warm body.

"I had extra security guys there all day. People were watching all the entrances and exits."

"Oh," Amber said, feeling a bit dumb.

Of course Hunter had planned everything out with precision. Unlike her.

She peeked up at Hunter and saw that he was rubbing his temple.

"So did security get what they needed to stop the Ross family?"

Hunter shook his head as though to clear it. He stepped away from her and she was unable to read his face. Was he angry?

"Yes," he said, rather absently. "At the very least, they won't be able to do any further damage. And my father will be pressing charges. I anticipate that either one or both of Kayla's parents will be doing jail time based on the evidence already collected."

"That's good, right?" Amber asked.

"Can we not talk about this anymore right now?"

Why wasn't he thanking her? Sure, she nearly messed up things in the beginning. But stopping Kayla from copying the papers had been brilliant!

"I kept the files safe."

She couldn't keep the indignation and disbelief out of her voice.

"The hallway was already being monitored. As I believe I told you earlier. We wanted to see if Kayla would actually be an accomplice without her mother looking over her shoulder."

Amber stood stock still, trying to work out what he was saying. Did he actually mean that she had hindered the investigation by preventing Kayla from copying the documents?

"But she was already helping her mom," she sputtered at last. "What does it matter what she did on her own?"

"Maybe nothing," Hunter said, his voice resigned. "Just forget it."

"No," Amber said, getting angry. "If you think that I messed up today, then I want to know about it."

Her eyes swung to the elevator door as a soft ding announced they had reached their floor.

Hunter smacked the stop button and Amber jerked back. His gorgeous green eyes were hard to see at the moment because he was squinting at her like she was insane.

"Can't you just drop this?" he asked, his voice low and dangerous.

"Why are you pushing me? It's like you want me to say something that I'll regret."

Chapter 15

Amber felt as though she might explode. It was as if all of her frustrations with Hunter's power struggles were rising to the surface. She was like a bottle of soda that had been dropped and shaken. One little twist and everything was going to spew out in a rush. She couldn't think straight. Even now he was trying to control things, to micro-manage both his emotions as well as her own.

"You are such a maniac," she said, her voice near shouting.

"You want me to be a delicate piece of artwork that can be admired and loved but always kept on a shelf!"

She leaned over to open the door, but Hunter grabbed her hand.

"We'll talk about this when we get back to the hotel," he growled.

"This is exactly what I'm talking about!" Amber shouted, yanking her hand back from his and pulling away.

"You even want to control when and how we argue! Do you get how annoying that is?"

Hunter had the nerve to gape at her. He slammed the elevator button and stalked out as soon as the doors opened. Walking swiftly down the corridor, he powered through the giant lobby doors, only stopping to say something quickly to the doorman on duty. And then he stalked off down the street, disappearing from view.

Amber stepped out of the elevator, still steaming mad. Even now, he was controlling what happened by walking away.

How dare he! She stormed down the corridor, fuming. No matter what she had or had not done, he was being childish by skulking off like that.

Why was she even doing this to herself? Anybody else would have put the brakes on before now. Maybe that was why Hunter had problems with relationships before, she thought viciously. He was acting like a spoiled brat.

The doorman spotted her and scurried to open the door.

"Excuse me, Mademoiselle," he said, speaking slowly in French. "The gentleman wanted to let you know that you may take the car back alone."

Amber had to struggle to follow his words but she got the point. Ironically, her French appeared to be progressing much better than her relationship with Hunter at the moment.

She thanked the doorman and found a safe place to cross. Traffic was thicker now. She would have been insane to try crossing in the middle of the street as she had before.

Amber could see the driver dozing in the front of the car. She tapped on the window and he jumped up in the seat, his eyes wild. Amber forced a smile as he rolled down the window. It wasn't the poor driver's fault that Hunter was being a jerk.

"Are you ready to leave, Mademoiselle?"

"No, thank you. But I'm planning on doing some shopping for the next hour or so. If you have another client, feel free to leave."

The driver looked dismayed.

"Have I insulted you, Mademoiselle?"

Amber shook her head emphatically and decided to be honest.

"I . . . um . . . I just had an argument with Mr. Webb. I'd rather take a walk and work off some of my anger."

"Ah!" the driver said knowingly. "A lover's spat. I am so sorry to hear of this, Mademoiselle. But please let me take you in the car."

"That really isn't necessary," Amber said, sighing.

The driver looked distressed. "But, Mademoiselle, I truly believe if I don't deliver you safe and sound, that this will be my very last time driving this car."

Oh, for goodness sake! Now I can't even get home on my own volition because Hunter the control freak is going to fire this poor man. She almost told the driver that she was terribly sorry. But she couldn't be that cruel. The man was literally wringing his hands.

"Fine," she said, giving up. She didn't need to feel guilty about this as well.

The driver's apparent relief was so visible that she was glad to not let her own pride stand in the way. After all, hadn't she simply wanted to let Hunter know that she could get home on her own? Shove it in his face that his fancy car was just a luxury rather than a necessity. Make him see how rich and spoiled he was?

As she passed the crowded subway, though, she bit her lip. She realized how glad she was she had not had to try to take it back to the hotel. Yes, she had taken it with Hunter before. But the confusing signs, crowds, and unfamiliar language had been tolerable only because she felt safe with Hunter.

She shoved that thought away. She wanted to remain angry with him. Strangely, though, she felt empty as her anger evaporated. All that was left was a vague sense of sadness. She stared out the window at the passing shops, galleries, and cafes.

What would happen if she and Hunter broke up? Was that where this was going? Is that what she wanted? She loved him. But she honestly didn't know if she could continue to live with him.

As they turned down one street, Amber saw a little studio advertising lessons in the art of stained glass. She quickly spoke to the driver and explained that she wanted him to stop. Just before she got out of the car, he pointed at her hair.

"The hair is very beautiful, Mademoiselle," he said, as though embarrassed, "but I wanted to remind you in case you had forgotten that you were still in disguise."

"Oh! Thanks for telling me." Amber yanked off the wig and removed the glasses.

She must have been really out of it not to have noticed they were still on. She looked around and realized that she must have left the briefcase somewhere at work. Sighing, she settled for leaving the wig and glasses on the seat next to her.

She pulled out her compact mirror to inspect her hair. Thankfully, her hair was still relatively neat in the low chignon that had kept it hidden beneath the wig.

"I won't be long," she told the driver. "It might be easier to circle around than to find a spot close by."

"No problem, Mademoiselle," he said. "I'll swing around once. If you are not ready by then, I'll try to find a spot. But take your time."

Amber waved him away and hurried down the street. The wind was bitterly cold. She couldn't believe that she had planned on trying to find her way back on the subway. That would have been one more reason for Hunter to assume that she never thought before she acted.

Her conscience chose that moment to give an opinion.

But he's right. You almost never think before you act.

Amber told her conscience to go take a hike. She wasn't going to allow herself to be reasonable right now.

As soon as she opened the wooden door, a pleasant bell rang out. Amber found herself smiling. The front of the studio was filled with lovely finished pieces ranging from the familiar flat pieces used in windows to gorgeous vases and lamps. In the back, a tall gentleman stepped away from a sketchpad.

"Bonjour, Mademoiselle," he greeted her, wiping his hands on a remarkably clean and tidy apron.

"Bonjour, Monsieur," Amber responded.

In halting French, while also pointing at the sign outside, she explained that she was interested in taking classes.

The gentlemen smiled at her warmly. He had bushy white eyebrows that matched the unruly thatch of curly white hair on his head.

"It is nice to see an American trying to learn our beautiful language," he said gently. "But allow me to speak English for you so that we have no mix up about the details of your questions."

Amber relaxed and grinned. "I promise I'll keep practicing."

"Excellent, Mademoiselle," the gentleman replied. "I am Monsieur Renaud and this is my studio and shop. Now, let us speak of the classes."

Amber wasn't sure how long she stayed in the shop as the master showed her some of his work and the small studio in the back where he held classes. She loved everything about the studio, including the smell of the freshly cut wooden frames and the sawdust on the workshop floor. She felt she could be very happy sitting in the cozy shop while the cold winds blew outside. Just before she left, she grabbed a brochure and schedule.

Not wanting to keep the driver waiting any longer, she hurried back out and found him double parked across the street. As he drove her back in the direction of the hotel, her stomach growled. She asked the driver to pull over so that she could buy a snack from a small shop. As she munched on her treat, she couldn't help but remember the dark, angry look on Hunter's face as he had stormed off.

Now that the chaos of the morning was behind her, she could think more clearly. For the first time that day, she allowed herself to think of how much stress Hunter must have experienced that day. To be truthful, she hadn't thought much about his needs at all. She tried to imagine having a business and knowing that somebody was trying to steal company secrets.

Okay, so maybe she should have given Hunter a little bit of slack. Yes, he had acted like a control freak. But his control freak nature had probably saved his parents a great amount of grief, not to mention who knows how much money. She still thought he should have been more considerate of her feelings. After all, she had acted with the best intentions. Well, mostly anyway.

By the time she got back to the hotel, Amber was in a weird mood. Her anger was mixed between herself and Hunter. Her mind looped in circles. She was getting a headache from thinking too much. Why couldn't things be like they were in the beginning?

You know why. What about the kidnapping? What about today? What would have happened if you walked in at the wrong time or if Kayla or her mother recognized you?

Amber slapped the button on the elevator. She didn't need her own conscience attacking her today.

Chapter 16

When she walked through the door, Amber found Hunter on the sofa. Just sitting there bent over with his elbows on his knees and his head in his hands. No newspaper or book or magazine. She glanced at the clock and saw that it was well after lunch.

She wanted to punish him for making her feel guilty. She reached out and purposely tossed her keys on the counter. She knew it bugged him when she wouldn't put them in the small silver bowl by the door.

Hunter winced. But he didn't say anything. He lifted his head, but she couldn't read his expression.

Had he really been sitting here this whole time? Maybe she shouldn't have stopped on the way for that croissant. She hadn't even thought about bringing something back for Hunter.

Her conscience jumped in with an unwanted opinion.

Hunter would not have forgotten you.

Amber picked up her keys and placed them gently in the silver bowl.

Hunter still hadn't said anything. She thought that this might be a world record for him. Was he waiting for her to start? What was she supposed to say?

Unexpectedly, she thought of a time when she was driving on the highway in her old beat up car. A small pebble had snapped up from the road and hit her windshield. The rock had left a tiny hole that she had been able to ignore for a little while. But then a small line started to form around the pock mark. The repair guy had explained that if she had waited much longer, the entire window would have eventually fractured.

That was how she was feeling right now. She knew that she and Hunter could smooth over today, but that small line was already starting to form in the relationship. Could Hunter sense that as well? Was that why he looked so forlorn? As though he suspected the flaw between them? Was it something that could be fixed?

"Do you mind if I change first?"

Hunter shook his head.

As she walked by, she could have sworn she heard his stomach growl. She quickened her pace. She was starting to get a little worried about Hunter. The control freak didn't just make sure that other people ate. She had never known him to skip a meal before. Ever.

In the bedroom, she quickly slipped out of her failed spy clothes and into a soft pair of jeans and a long sleeved tee shirt. The room was a bit chilly so she added a thick pair of socks. Then she padded back into the living room.

A fire would have felt nice, but there was no way she was going to suggest one. She suddenly felt like crying. As much as she felt that she and Hunter were ill-matched, she felt nauseated thinking of splitting up. Even if she was the one to initiate it.

She sat next to Hunter, feeling the huge space between them, both physical and emotionally. Swallowing hard, she forced herself to speak.

"I'm sorry that I almost screwed everything up today," she said softly. "And I shouldn't have yelled at you. At least not then. I guess I was just caught up in my own drama."

Hunter turned to face her. He looked defeated.

"This isn't just about today, is it?"

Amber sighed, realizing he was right. Something had snapped today. Maybe even before today.

"No. I suppose not."

"When did you get the wig?"

Amber couldn't look him in the eyes.

"A few days ago," she whispered.

Hunter nodded silently. He returned to his previous position. Elbows balanced on knees and head clasped in both hands.

Amber suddenly realized how painful deception with the wig must feel like to him. She had told herself that she was only avoiding a fight. But her secret was another wedge between them.

"What do you want to do?"

She had never heard his voice like that. Despondent.

Amber blinked back tears.

"I love you, Hunter. I just don't know if I can live with your control freak nature. Maybe we should take a little breather. I need some time to think."

Hunter sat up and Amber was shocked to see that his eyes were glistening. He blinked hard and shook his head.

"I love you too, Amber," he said, his voice shaky.

"This doesn't have to be the end," Amber said quickly. "This will be good for both of us."

"Sure," Hunter said, not sounding convinced. He stood and walked to the closet.

"I thought this might happen. Just in case, I packed a suitcase."

Amber felt like she had been struck in the chest.

"Oh! I didn't mean . . ."

What had she done? Where was he going? For that matter, where would she go? She couldn't expect to stay here at his expense.

See. You don't think things through.

"I want you to stay here. I'll stay with my parents until . . . well, until you decide what you want to do."

Amber gaped at him. This was more generous than she could have imagined. After all, she was the one asking for a break.

"This has nothing to do with your work at the office," he said firmly. "My mom loves working with you. And continue using the car service."

Amber tried to object. "That's nice of you to offer, but . . ."

Hunter cut her off before she could continue.

"You already hate me. So I'm just going to go ahead and pull another control freak move on you. The driver has already been paid in advance."

Hunter was now moving through the room swiftly, grabbing his phone, his briefcase, and the suitcase. He gave her one last look before his mouth quivered. He turned away from her, but not before one tear slid down his cheek.

And then he opened the door and slipped through without another glance back.

Chapter 17

What have I done?

Amber Holloway stared at the shut door, stunned that the love of her life had just walked out with a suitcase.

And the worst thing about this situation?

This was her doing. She asked for "some time apart." She questioned whether she could continue to be in a relationship with him.

But she hadn't expected everything to happen so fast. The enormity of the last half hour sucked the breath out of her.

No matter that Hunter's control freak nature led to all of this. She loved him. The enormity of what she had done overwhelmed her.

Her conscience berated her.

You never think anything through. Hunter was right about that. Maybe you could have worked it out. Maybe you shouldn't have pushed him.

Amber fidgeted. She pounded her fists on the leather sofa. She stood and paced around the hotel suite.

She half expected to see Hunter pop his head around a corner. His presence lingered everywhere. The leather chair he preferred in the mornings. The sofa where they cuddled in the evenings. His bedroom.

Amber felt out of place. Who was she to be in such an extravagant hotel? Only months earlier she had been on the verge of getting evicted from her tiny studio apartment. Before that, she had lived with her mother in a trailer. Back then food had been a luxury.

And now? The furnishings and the decorations all screamed wealth and opulence. All of this was the courtesy of Hunter who had never lacked for any material thing.

She was like Cinderella who got chosen and then decided she didn't like the life of a privileged princess. Okay, that wasn't the best comparison. She did enjoy having a nice place to live and not worrying about where the money for food was coming from.

Correction. She had enjoyed eating regularly and not worrying about money everyday. But Hunter was not going to support her indefinitely. Not when she had just told him that she couldn't live with him in spite of her love.

A sick compulsion made Amber walk into his room. She sank onto the bed. Hunter's scent, a mixture of paint, turpentine, and soap, clung to the pillows and bedding.

She ran her fingers along the comforter and was struck by the respect he had shown her. In spite of providing her with free housing,food, and even clothing, Hunter had never pressured her for sex. Sure, they had kissed passionately. But she had always felt respected.

What had she given up? She already ached at his absence.

Hunter with his green, mesmerizing eyes. Hunter with that stubborn lock of hair that always fell so alluringly over his eyes.

Her conscience added to the list.

Don't forget how he saved you twice in one week. Before he even knew you. And later, he saved you from freezing to death in the middle of nowhere after a kidnapping.

Amber jerked upright and bolted from the room. But there was nowhere in the hotel suite that was safe from his presence. She stalked to the full-sized refrigerator, thinking to get a bottle of cold water. She yanked the door open and stood, transfixed.

Several paper sacks, carefully labeled with her name, lined one of the shelves.

Her breath caught. Had he calculated things were over when she didn't come straight back to the hotel after the fight? She pictured him coming to the worst possible conclusion and then planning a way to take care of her needs. Even when he must have been hurting.

A shudder worked its way up her spine. The first fat, hot tear rolled down her cheek. She knew he hadn't wanted to break up. She had seen the unfamiliar slump of his shoulders as he left. The few quick tears he tried to hide from her.

Amber slammed the refrigerator and shuffled back to the sofa in a watery blur. She remembered hearing Hunter's stomach growling just before she ended things. Which meant that even though they parted angrily that morning, he had managed to subvert his own needs and wants in order to make sure that she was taken care of.

For all of her anger at Hunter's control issues, she couldn't fault him for his generosity and caring. Nobody had ever watched over her like him.

But there was the rub. Hunter didn't know when to stop. His caring went so far as to be smothering.

If this was the right thing to do, why did it hurt so badly?

Heartache. She had never understood the term until today.

What an unpleasant surprise that the word was an accurate representation of the physical pain in her chest. As though someone had ripped her heart out, flung it on the floor and stomped on it for good measure.

She curled into a ball, the tears scalding her cheeks.

Why had she done this?

Even now, for all of her frustration his control freak nature, she wanted to curl up against his chest and have Hunter comfort her.

Chapter 18

Hunter's legs didn't want to work properly. Stepping away from the love of his life was like trying to walk with concrete blocks attached to his feet. In place of his heart was a painful lump.

As he passed the front desk, he saw the day manager glance away with sympathy. Hunter had filled the man in as to why he might not be showing up any time soon. Of course, he had also wanted to make sure that any hotel bills, including meals, were paid in advance.

Hunter tried to preserve his self dignity. He hoisted his shoulders and attempted a smile. But his traitor lips had other ideas. He felt them trembling. Ducking his head, he hurried out the door and into the bustling street. The blast of cold air helped dry the few tears that had sneaked out of his eyes. Twisting, he turned to search for the private car.

Okay, time to get your emotions in check. Do not cry. Repeat. Do not cry.

"Good afternoon, Monsieur Webb," the young, lanky driver called out.

"Good afternoon, Pierre. Thanks for waiting."

Hunter allowed Pierre to take his single suitcase and stow it in the trunk. He slid in the back seat. Pierre knew all the basic details, of course, since Hunter had spoken to him by phone to make arrangements for Amber's future transportation needs. Now a strained tension filled the car.

Pierre settled into the driver's seat and eased the car into late afternoon traffic.

"Where to, Monsieur?"

"My parent's house, thank you."

Hunter caught Pierre's eye as he glanced back in the rear view mirror.

"I'm sorry if this is awkward for you, Pierre," he said carefully. "And I appreciate your discretion."

"Absolutely, Monsieur Webb. I'm so sorry that you are in this difficult position."

Sitting there, Hunter realized that this was the most personal conversation he had ever had with the driver. In another place and time, he would have already made friends with the man.

"Thank you. And I'd like it if you called me Hunter."

"Pardon, Monsieur?"

Hunter warily shook his head.

"Please, let's not be so formal. You can't be much older than me. And I could really use a friend right now."

He paused, considering.

"Unless you think I'm some sort of monster that deserves having my girlfriend dump me."

Pierre shook his head.

"Not at all. Your girlfriend is rather, um, spirited." His ears reddened. "And nice, of course."

Hunter willed up a small smile. "Spirited is an apt description, I suppose."

Pierre nodded, his attention on the traffic.

Hunter sank back against the seat, exhausted from the stress of trying to appear normal when he felt like his whole world was cracking apart. He couldn't believe he had been about to ask Amber to marry him.

He stared out the window, clenching his fists to maintain control. He could do this. After all, he was a certifiable control freak.

Walking through the doors of his old home felt comforting. He had stayed here from time to time, of course. But this felt different. This time he felt as though he was a small child running home with skinned knees.

Though his family had moved to the United States when he was still very young, they had not wanted to give up the family home. When they returned to Paris, everything was as they left it.

A staff of cleaners had simply removed all the furniture coverings before polishing the wood, airing out carpets, and washing linens. Hunter's twin bed still had the same blue striped sheets and comforter. Most of his toys and stuffed animals had been packed up and stored somewhere in the attic. However, sitting in an antique rocking chair in the corner, there was his beloved gray stuffed rabbit with one of its button eyes missing.

He walked over and got it now, gathering it in his arms as he sank onto the bed. Hugging the rabbit against his chest, he curled into a ball, finally letting himself cry for the first time since he walked out of the hotel room.

Chapter 19

All out weeping sessions never made Amber feel better. Right now, for instance, her nose was so stopped up that she had to gasp for breath between every few sobs. Disgusting snot oozed from her nose and soaked both her face and tee shirt. The clammy snot was the breaking point. She stumbled to the bathroom for tissues, trying not to look at Hunter's bedroom.

After cleaning herself up and washing her face in cold water, she changed into pajama pants and a fresh tee shirt. She grabbed a pillow and a blanket from her bed and retreated back to the living room. She plopped onto the couch and stretched out. He short frame fit perfectly. Spent from crying, she fell into a fitful sleep.

Hours later, she woke to knocking. Untangling herself from the blanket, she shuffled to the door. Through the peep hole, she recognized one of the bellhops. He was carrying a food tray.

Amber opened the door.

"I'm sorry," she said in French. "I didn't order anything."

The bellhop shrugged and fired off a rapid reply in French.

From the little bit she could understand, Hunter had arranged for the food to be delivered.

Sighing, Amber stepped back and allowed him to enter. She was hungry, after all, and the food would be thrown away if she sent it back. She asked the bellhop to wait and reached for her purse. But he waved her away with a smile, telling her it was not necessary. At least that's what she thought he said.

After he left, Amber opened the tray and wanted to cry again. Hunter had chosen pizza, a bowl of fresh fruit, and croissants. All her favorites. All things that could go in the fridge and be eaten later if she wasn't hungry at the moment.

Why did he have to be so considerate? When she was with him, she had considered this sort of thing his being a control freak. But what was in it for him now? He knew he was risking making her angry.

Her conscience had a reply all ready.

He wanted to make sure that you had something decent to eat tonight. Just like he made sure that you had a place to live and transportation to work every day.

Groaning, Amber pushed those thoughts out of her head. She was about to convince herself that she was the problem. Finding the remote for the television, she turned it on, watching a silly French sitcom while she ate. She wanted to be distracted.

But all she could think about was how Hunter loved to make up inappropriate translations for the characters on the show to make her laugh. Or the way that they snuggled together on the sofa.

Why was she thinking of all the good times?

Amber willed herself to consume an entire slice of pizza and a small portion of fruit. The rest of the plate she stuck in the refrigerator for later. Cold pizza for breakfast might be nice. After putting everything away, she padded to the bathroom to take a shower.

Once she got in, though, she remembered the first day that Hunter brought her to the hotel. Everything had seemed perfect then. She had been so thrilled not to have to wait for him to return from Paris after his internship. Was everything going to serve up a reminder of what she was giving up?

Amber turned up the hot water, letting the stinging water on her flesh distract her from her memories. Her skin was red and wrinkled like a prune when she finally toweled off.

Back in the living room, she heard a buzz indicating she had a text. She stared at the phone as though it might explode. It buzzed again, making her jump.

You're being ridiculous. How do you know that it's Hunter?

But she did know. Further, she realized that she wanted him to contact her. Still, it took several minutes to work up the courage to pick up the phone.

You could ignore it. Or wait until tomorrow when your emotions are not so raw.

Who was she kidding? She clicked on the icon.

I know I shouldn't be bothering you. But need to know if you are okay?

Amber clutched her phone, trying not to give in to the temptation to return a message. Honestly, she didn't know what to say. Everything was still so muddled in her head.

She put the phone on the coffee table. She flipped through the television channels. Finally, she couldn't take it anymore. She tapped out a brief message and clicked the send button.

I'm still processing . . . How is the situation at work?

The phone buzzed again.

Don't worry about work. It will all get sorted out.

And . . . I know this isn't the right time . . . but you looked incredible in your spy gear.

Amber groaned. That would have been nice to hear earlier in the day. Now it just added to her confusion. She tapped in a reply.

Wrong time. Wrong place. But thank you.

Amber waited for the phone to buzz. Instead it was silent. Had Hunter expected a different response? She stared at the phone, willing it to buzz again.

She checked the time. Two minutes had passed. It felt like twenty. She threw the phone on the table and clicked on the television. She flipped through the stations mindlessly.

Finally the phone buzzed again.

No matter what you decide, I still love you. Have a good night sleep.

Amber felt her eyes sting. If she didn't stop this, she was going to be bawling like a baby again. She was already fighting the impulse to tell Hunter that she had made a huge mistake. All she could think of was having his arms wrapped around her.

Her fingers shook as she typed in the next message.

I still love you too. Go to bed. You have an early morning at the gallery.

Staring at her reply, Amber was struck by how much it sounded like something Hunter would say. She pushed her phone away and tried to go to sleep.

But for at least an hour, she found herself staring at the phone, willing it to buzz one more time. This was crazy, she thought. She was the one who needed time alone. So why was she craving Hunter's attention? At long last, she drifted off to sleep again.

Chapter 20

Hunter twisted beneath the sheets of his small childhood bed. He couldn't call in sick again the next day. If nothing else, moping in his bedroom only made him feel more pathetic about his life.

He couldn't believe he had been on the verge of asking Amber to marry him. What an idiot he had been! And it was all his fault. That was the worst part. He couldn't even blame her for how she felt.

No, this was his control freak nature. What Amber didn't understand, couldn't understand, were his private demons. And why would he share those with anyone? That terrible day still haunted him. He shook his head violently. No. He refused to let the memories surface.

Groaning, Hunter stared at his childhood ceiling. He reached over to turn off the lamp and the entire space above his head glowed with hundreds of stars. He remembered his mother climbing the ladder to stick them on one by one all those years ago. Even now as an adult, he was thrilled to see them shining in the dark.

He was sure that Amber would enjoy them. But no. Not now.

Stop being a wimp! Sure, you messed up. Badly. But that doesn't mean you have to roll over and play dead. Be a man. Figure this out.

Hunter flung his covers off, bolted upright, and switched the lamp back on. He got out of bed and carefully placed the gray stuffed rabbit back in the rocking chair. His conscience was right. He wasn't a helpless little kid anymore. Walking to his bedroom door, he cracked it and made sure nobody was in the hallway before slipping into the bathroom to wash his face.

Wow. He wasn't looking so good. His eyes were puffy and red from crying. Good thing that Amber couldn't see him like this. He swallowed hard and returned to the bedroom. This time he simply sat on the edge of the bed, unwilling to let himself just lie down and wallow in self pity.

He thought about how he had waited and waited for Amber the day she broke up with him. Pierre had finally relented and revealed that she had stopped at an art gallery on the way back. Had she been there before? Was there something in that visit that he should understand? If only he could question her without risking her temper.

Finally inspiration hit. Leaping up again, he foraged in the side table for a marker. When he didn't find anything, he slipped into the living room. There was only a single lamp shining in the front room, meaning that his parents had already gone bed.

Hunter finally located a black marker in his mother's small desk. Filled with new purpose, he strode back to his bedroom and searched in the closet for an old extra pillow. Then he sat down and sketched Amber's face directly on the fabric.

He propped the pillow up on the headboard and addressed it sternly.

"Why did you stop at the art gallery? Why was it so important that day?"

He pulled out the crumpled paper brochure and schedule he had stuck in the bedside table drawer. Of course it hadn't been all wadded up when Pierre gave it to him.

At first Hunter thought Amber had purposely left it in the car to taunt him. But now he realized that Pierre was probably right. He could see Amber getting distracted and carelessly tossing the papers on the seat when she got in the car. Messy might as well have been her middle name.

Smoothing out the wrinkles, he studied the advertisement. Stained glass art?

"Are you bored, Amber? Are you missing your art that badly?"

Amber's likeness stared back at him.

"Giving me the silent treatment, are you?"

Hunter pondered his own current life. Yes, his hours at the art gallery were crazy. But he had chunks of the day where he was encouraged to sketch or paint if there wasn't an important client to take around the city.

"So I've been selfish by not considering your artistic needs?"

Pillow Amber mocked him.

"Okay, I can understand that. But why didn't you tell me?"

As he stared at Pillow Amber, Hunter knew exactly why the real Amber hadn't said anything. She felt guilty that he gave her everything. And one thing he knew about Amber was that she was selfless to the point of hurting herself.

Hunter sighed. Of course he knew that about her. He had just gotten so caught up in the fantasy of their living together in the hotel. It was almost like they were a married couple. Except for the sex, of course. He wanted to wait until they were wed.

"How do I fix this for you, Amber? Will taking classes be enough?"

Hunter stared at Pillow Amber.

She stared back as though he was crazy.

"You're tough as sandpaper," he muttered at last. "Okay, I'll agree to the shrink if you agree to the classes. Deal?"

Picking up his cell phone, Hunter mustered up his courage. He needed to proceed carefully, having promised his parents to give her some space. But what he needed to tell her could not wait. Especially if he wasn't going to chicken out.

Chapter 21

Amber had lucked out by having several scheduled days off after the breakup. She wasn't sure how she would have handled coming in the day after. Even walking in today felt awkward.

A handwritten note with directions for the day's research waited on her desk. The request was particularly involved. Amber didn't have much time to think about Hunter as she got busy.

At lunch time, she grabbed the sack lunch Hunter had prepared for her and brought it back to her desk. She spent a minute or two feeling sad as she contemplated his handwriting on the bag. But Mrs. Webb had insisted that the research be finished before their meeting that afternoon.

Amber dumped the sandwich and fruit on her desk and got back to work. Finally, around two o'clock that afternoon, she gathered her things and walked down the hall to Mrs. Webb's office.

"How are you, dear?" The elegant woman greeted her with a warm hug and a look of sympathy.

"Hunter told us what happened. I hope you don't mind, but that's why I made sure you stayed busy this morning."

Amber flushed. Of course Hunter's family knew. How else would he have explained having to stay at their house?

"I suppose it did help," she admitted. "I certainly wasn't thinking about our problems."

Mrs. Webb folded her hands on her desk and leaned forward.

"I know it really isn't any of my business, dear," she said frankly. "But Mr. Webb and I already love you as a daughter. Please let me know if there is anything we can do to help either of you."

Amber blinked away tears. She adored Hunter's parents.

"I do love Hunter," she confessed. "It's just that I feel confined with his controlling nature."

Mrs. Webb nodded her head. "I can see how that could be quite stifling. No matter what Hunter's intentions are, he needs to learn to let you have your freedom."

She smiled. "Even if it's a scary transition for him."

"Thank you. You and your family have been so kind and generous."

"I hope that you'll stay in Paris while you decide what to do," Mrs. Webb said. "I would be lost without your contributions to the Foundation."

"Of course. I love the work that we're doing."

"Fine, then let's go over the research you were working on this morning. I'd like to start on a presentation for our top investors."

Amber let herself be drawn in by the comfort of her job. Before she knew it, the day was complete and she heard employees start to leave their offices, calling to each other in the corridor.

"Oh, I've kept you much too long!" Mrs. Webb glanced up at the clock.

"It's quite all right," Amber said, thinking of another long evening by herself.

"Why don't we grab dinner together? Just us girls? Mr. Webb is meeting Hunter at the gallery for an early dinner."

"You shouldn't change your plans on my account," Amber protested weakly.

"Nonsense! I was going to have leftovers and putter around the house until the boys got home. I'd much rather have dinner out with you."

Amber had worried that Mrs. Webb might spend the evening trying to get her to rethink her break from Hunter. Instead, Mrs. Webb kept her laughing by telling outrageous stories from her own past dating.

At the end of the evening, Amber felt remarkably relaxed and upbeat. She was sure that some of the love stories had been exaggerated, but the evening was surprisingly enjoyable.

"I almost didn't date him," Mrs. Webb said, referencing her husband as she slathered butter on a slice of bread.

"Really? Why not?"

"I thought he was gay." Mrs. Webb spoke with complete seriousness.

"You're putting me on!"

"Nope. It's true."

"Even though he was asking you out?"

Mrs. Webb smiled. "One of the boys in our class had a huge crush on Mr. Webb."

"And he didn't know about the crush. Your husband, I mean?"

Mrs. Webb put a hand to her chin as she thought.

"At the time I had no idea. Now? I don't think he had a clue."

"So how did you end up going out with him?" Amber cut off a tiny sliver of perfectly cooked steak.

"I got tired of refusing him." Mrs. Webb laughed. "Every day after class, he blocked the doorway and ask me out. I agreed to one date if he promised to stop pestering me."

"That must have been some date."

"Let's just say that I discovered that he was not gay."

Amber laughed and the two continued a congenial meal together. She had such a lovely time that she was in a good frame of mind once she got back to the hotel.

After a shower, she donned her baggy pajama bottoms and soft tee shirt and relaxed on the sofa. She grabbed an empty notebook and began a decision tree.

You are such a nerd!

She drew two columns and started filling them in.

REASONS TO BREAK UP WITH HUNTER

He is a control freak.

He will always be a control freak.

REASONS TO STAY WITH HUNTER

I fell in love with him just as he is.

He can't help his control freak nature.

His control freak nature saved me – three times!

He makes me feel beautiful.

I love his gorgeous green eyes.

He overlooks my bad habits.

He feeds me even when I reject him.

He gave up this hotel suite for me.

Staring at the list, Amber gasped. She ripped the page from the notebook, crumpled it into a tiny ball, and tossed it under the sofa.

So much for the good mood. Now she was sobbing again.

Chapter 22

After several minutes of crying, Amber made herself get up off the couch. She was determined not to allow herself to wallow in self pity. She walked to the bathroom to blow her nose and wipe her face. She made herself stare at the lonely bed for a full minute without crying. Then she quickly stripped her clothes and turned the water on in the shower. Maybe she could wash away the despair that clung to her.

When she returned to the living room, she checked her phone and saw that she had a few new texts from Hunter.

Found some of your stuff in the car. Can I call you?

Amber bit her lip and typed her response before she could change her mind.

Yes.

Her phone rang almost instantly.

"That was quick," she said as a greeting.

"I was afraid you might change your mind."

"I haven't made any decisions yet. So I hope that isn't why you're calling."

There was a brief pause on the other end of the line and Amber realized she might have been too abrupt. Well, that was kind of the point wasn't it? Still, she did agree to the call.

"Sorry. I didn't intend to sound so harsh."

"Um . . . I suppose I had it coming. But for the record, I did call to discuss something else. I found your wig and stuff in the car. Also a schedule and brochure on a stained glass art course."

Amber grabbed her purse and looked inside. She could have sworn she had put the papers in there. Of course, she had been flustered before she got out of the car. Now that she thought about it, she remembered not wanting to put her sticky fingers from the croissant on the schedule.

"Amber?"

"Sorry, I spaced out a second. I hadn't noticed that the art stuff was missing. The course looked interesting. I thought it might fill the time when I'm not working."

"That's what I wanted to talk about," Hunter said, sounding nervous. "I thought we could make a deal."

"What kind of deal?"

Amber's back stiffened. He better not offer to pay for the courses in return for getting back together.

"It's not what you think," Hunter said quickly. "I . . . um . . . I would be willing to go to a . . . well . . . a psychologist if you agree to accept a gift of some classes."

What? Okay, she definitely had not seen that coming.

"Are you serious? You're willing to see a psychologist?"

"Yes," Hunter said firmly. "If there is even a sliver of hope of getting you back, I'll spill my guts to anybody."

"Hunter, that's great! I know that this is such a huge step for you."

On the outside, she gushed. But inside, Amber tried to keep her enthusiasm in check. What if the therapy didn't work? What if Hunter couldn't open up even to a professional?

"So you'll accept the classes?" Hunter still sounded anxious.

"I don't get how me taking classes is a good thing for you," Amber said, puzzled. "I mean, I totally want you to see someone. But what's in it for you paying for my classes?"

Hunter mumbled something.

"Can you repeat that? I couldn't make out what you said."

"I said that I feel guilty," Hunter said in a slightly louder voice. "I brought you here and now you probably feel stuck and . . ."

"Hunter, stop. You don't have to feel guilty. I don't know of any jilted boyfriend who would be this kind and caring. Really, paying for the classes isn't necessary."

"Please. Amber."

Just two words. But Hunter's voice had such longing and sadness that Amber relented.

"Okay, Hunter. I don't get it. But if spending more money on me makes a difference, I'll allow you to pay for some courses."

"Thanks, Amber. You don't know how happy that makes me!"

Amber had to admit that he did sound happier. Of course, this was more evidence that he really did need to see a therapist.

"I'm happy that you're happy."

"I have to go now," Hunter said, sounding reluctant.

"I promised Mom and Dad that I wouldn't stalk you. Sweet dreams tonight."

"I'm really proud of this step you're taking, Hunter. Take care of yourself, okay?"

"I'll do whatever you want me to." Hunter's voice sounded muffled. "Anything at all."

"Goodnight, Hunter." Amber swiped at her eyes. "Sweet dreams."

She forced herself to hang up quickly. Cradling the phone, she thought about Hunter's stunning proposition. Would he really see a therapist? Would it make a difference?

She felt even more confused than before. Quite frankly, Hunter's reaction to this whole breakup was throwing her for a loop. For the first time since she met him, he seemed unsure of himself. She sighed, knowing she was going to have another restless night of sleep.

Chapter 23

The enormous wooden doors, with sunken glass panels, were just as Hunter remembered them. He stood across the street, taking in the stone facade of the building's exterior. He craned his head up to admire the weathered stone gargoyles that had both fascinated and terrified him as a child. And here he was again, as an adult. He had no choice coming here before.

Hunter drew a determined breath, crossed the street, and pulled open the heavy doors. His shoes tapped on the marbled floors. He checked for the name of the psychologist and then chose to take the spiral stairs to the third floor rather than wait for the elevator.

Images of his past flitted through his mind. His mother's warm hand. The rhythmic vibration in his fingers as he dragged his toy action figure across the black, curlicued hand railing. The pile of small toys arranged on rugs in the offices of the child psychologists. The staring contests between himself and the doctors. His mother's frustration.

Each week his mother sought someone knew. An older therapist. A younger therapist. A pleasant woman with long blond hair. A man who laughed too much. And finally, at her wits end, his mother had taken him to see one last specialist.

Hunter would not have cared had he known that the man was an adult psychologist. But, surprisingly, Hunter had been afraid of him from the very beginning. This man did not give him any toys. He bade him sit in the adult chair. And then he asked Hunter's mother to wait in the other room.

"Don't leave me!" Hunter had cried.

But his mother, perhaps exasperated, was willing to try anything. She walked out without even looking at her son.

"What a clever little boy you are, Hunter. You've been having fun with my colleagues. They don't know what to make of you."

Hunter stared at the tops of his shoes. The chair he sat in was so large that his legs could not dangle over the edge.

He tried to look at the man's eyes. But this man had no interest in the staring game. He looked everywhere except at Hunter.

The doctor had opened up a dish shaped like a beehive. From inside, he pulled out a wrapped caramel.

Hunter pretended not to notice the candy. But his mouth watered.

"My wife says I eat too many sweets." The doctor took his time unwrapping the confection.

Hunter couldn't pull his gaze away as the doctor placed the sweet on his tongue.

The man took his time. He chewed slowly, smiling and murmuring until the candy was finally swallowed. And then, almost as if it was an afterthought, he reached into the jar and brought out another piece.

He stood and turned to the window, the shiny gold wrapper winking in his hand as he moved.

"You're very good at hiding what's in your head."

The doctor turned and casually moved around the room.

Hunter couldn't stop himself from looking at the candy. When the doctor walked by and tossed it into his lap, he snatched it up without thinking. But he waited until the man stared out the window again before tearing open the wrapper.

The doctor tapped a blue pen against the window sill. He fiddled with the long cord that opened and closed the blinds.

Hunter popped the candy into his mouth. He worked the sticky glob around his mouth and chewed the softening edges. He watched the doctor warily.

The doctor spun his chair around. One. Two. Three times.

Hunter wondered if his own chair could twirl like that.

"Are you afraid that you did something wrong, Hunter? Because your parents think you are simply mourning the loss of your pet."

Hunter had gasped, suddenly afraid that this man could see inside his head. He climbed off the chair, ran to the rubbish bin, and spit out the remainder of his candy.

"I want to help you, Hunter."

The doctor was not looking at him. Had not even moved his head. But that was even scarier. His powers worked even from a distance.

"No matter what you think you did wrong, you have built it up out of proportion."

Hunter backed away, terrified. He grabbed at the door.

"Why don't you think about coming back to see me next week?"

But the following week, Hunter pitched a royal fit when his mother asked him to get in the car. She tried waiting him out. But he had proven quite stubborn. As soon as she pulled the car back into the garage, he became calm and subdued. However, the moment the car eased into the street, Hunter began to wail. He cried until he could scarcely breathe.

By the time she reached the office, his mother was crying with him.

She picked him up, carried him inside the office, and deposited him on the floor of the psychologist. The doctor sat at his desk, calmly eating his caramel candies while Hunter thrashed on the office floor, working himself up until he drooled all over himself.

At the end of the session, the doctor approached Hunter on his knees and informed him that their time was up.

Hunter instantly stopped wailing. He sat up and allowed the doctor to help wipe the tears and snot from his face. Once Hunter was presentable, the doctor opened his special jar and counted out three caramels.

"Do you think that you can wait in the other room while I speak with your mother?"

Hunter nodded solemnly. And thirty minutes later, his ordeal with psychologists ended.

Now, as an adult, Hunter wanted to flee the building. But getting Amber back would be impossible if he didn't even try facing his ghosts.

The patient waiting room resembled any other physician's office. There were several worn leather sofas to sit on as well as an abundance of magazines stacked neatly on a long, low glass coffee table. The counter was stocked with coffee, tea, and bottled water. Hunter checked in and sank on the sofa. He was exactly five minutes early, as was his custom.

No one else was in the room. That made him feel a little better. Still, he caught himself jangling his legs nervously. He felt like an idiot being scared of a psychologist. Fortunately, he didn't have to wait long.

The doctor, a slender man in his mid sixties, approached from a side door. He had thick, gray hair, combed to the side. Smiling, he extended a hand.

"Hello. I'm Dr. Gautier."

Hunter stared into the eyes of the same doctor he had seen as a kid. He tried to hide his surprise. Forcing a smile, he jerked his hand out to shake hands. But he was rattled. Had his mom arranged this on purpose?

After offering Hunter a chair, the doctor sat down across from him, crossing his legs. He wore simple corduroy trousers, a pale-blue button down shirt, and a dark-blue sweater vest. The small office appeared remarkably the same as it had when Hunter was just a kid. Even the beehive candy jar was still on the desk.

Dr. Gautier smiled.

"I wasn't sure if you would remember me. Your mother thought you might be upset."

Just like before, the doctor reached for his candy jar.

"I assured her that you were probably past pitching a temper tantrum."

Hunter wanted to be insulted. Instead, he felt an ease he hadn't expected. For the first time since he allowed his mother to make the appointment for him, he actually relaxed.

"I've set aside my demon theatrics. I should thank you for treating me so nicely when I was such a little monster."

Dr. Gautier unwrapped his candy with the same deliberate movement as all those years ago.

"I always wondered if I pushed you too far too early. Perhaps you would have eventually opened up."

Hunter laughed.

"I'm afraid that wasn't going to happen, Dr. Gautier. I was determined that nobody was going to learn my secrets. I only grew afraid because . . ."

He broke off, embarrassed to say the rest.

But Dr. Gautier simply sat there, his eyes on his own fingers as he patiently waited for a response. Perhaps he was used to having people talk in fits and starts.

"I was convinced that you had super powers and could see into my brain."

His deep blue eyes crinkling at the corners, Dr. Gautier smiled delightedly.

"Ah! A super power! That would have been a wonderful tool to have in my bag of tricks."

"So, anyway, my mom thinks that whatever happened when I was a kid might have made me more controlling than is appropriate."

"Do you think that you are too controlling?" Dr. Gautier gazed at him serenely.

The question caught Hunter off guard.

"Well, um . . . I get accused of it a lot. So I suppose so."

"But how do you feel when you are actually engaged in the so-called controlling manner?" Dr. Gautier persisted. "Do you think that your actions are appropriate at the time?"

"Most of the time, I think I'm doing the right thing," Hunter confessed.

"Sometimes I don't get why people react like they do. I mean, sometimes I do exert some pressure to get my way. But most of my problems with my girlfriend surface when I'm trying to do things to keep her safe."

Dr. Gautier nodded his head. "You mother told me that your friend has experienced actual danger in the recent past. I find it reasonable for you to be antsy. The question is the degree to which you are offering your protection for her."

Hunter shook his head. "I don't get it. I limited her involvement in this one situation and she went nuts."

Dr. Gautier tapped his fingers together thoughtfully.

"And what level, say on a scale of one to ten, would you have rated her level of mortal danger in that particular scenario?"

Hunter flushed. "Well, there probably wasn't a huge element of danger."

Dr. Gautier wasn't letting him off that easily. "So, the number would be . . . ?"

Hunter sighed. "I suppose a one or a two. But anything could have happened."

He wished Dr. Gautier would say something else. Instead, the man placed the candy in his mouth. He closed his eyes and chewed, his expression serene.

Hunter wondered how much of this was theatrics and how much was the man's genuine love of sweets.

"I'm afraid I'm still addicted to these." Dr. Gautier fished another piece of candy from the bright yellow pot.

"Care for one yourself?"

Hunter held out his hand. He felt an urge to fill the gap in conversation.

"I never told anyone what really happened. You were right that day. There was something that I was afraid to tell anyone."

Dr. Gautier relaxed back in his chair, serenely chewing another piece of caramel.

Hunter kept his own piece in his hand, moving it from palm to palm.

"I wasn't supposed to leave the pasture. A single gate opens to a small road connecting to the village center."

Hunter risked a look up. But Dr. Gautier was calmly eating his candy, his hands quiet on his lap.

"That day wasn't the first. I had sneaked out before. Not far. I was too afraid for that."

Hunter clenched his hands as he allowed himself to relive that day. It was winter and he had woken snuggled up against his puppy. His grandparents were spending the morning working on a giant crossword puzzle in a corner of the kitchen near the wood burning stove. It was a Saturday and his parents were traveling to a wedding.

He found himself telling Dr. Gautier all the details while he relived each scene in his head.

He had jogged down the hall in fluffy bear slippers, wearing thick, striped pajamas. He had paused only to put on his boots and coat so that he could let Coco relieve himself in the back yard. Then they came inside for breakfast, the puppy squatting eagerly at his feet as Hunter dropped bits of pancakes and bacon under the table.

Afterward, he had dressed quickly, eager to play in the small amount of snow dusting the ground outside. At some point, he had seen the gate in the distance. Coco hadn't been with him the last excursion. He couldn't remember why. Whatever the reason, Coco didn't want to stray outside the gate.

"It was as though he knew it was wrong," Hunter said softly, mangling the piece of candy in his hand.

"I yelled at him at first. And he just looked at me with his little head turned up to the side like he didn't understand what I was asking."

Hunter flashed back to Coco sitting there, his beautiful brown coat ruffling in the sharp wind. Those soft brown eyes stared at him curiously. Coco was his best friend in the whole world.

"I don't know why I did it," he whispered. "I was so angry because I wanted to go exploring with him. And he just sat there being stubborn. And then, I picked up my foot and nudged him. But he wouldn't budge. I got even angrier. And then I kicked him."

Hunter's head dropped in his hands and he could feel tears spilling down his cheeks.

"I kicked my best friend. And he made the worst sound and darted out the gate. I started to run after him. But he didn't stop. And I was too frightened to follow him all the way down the road."

Hunter started to sob. "I don't even know if he survived or not. Every day I went to the gate and looked, hoping he would try to come back. That was the worst part of all. Not knowing if he was dead or alive. And knowing that it was all my fault."

He felt a soft hand on his shoulder. Dr. Gautier gave his arm a small squeeze and handed him a box of tissues.

He looked up, his chest tight. He expected to see horror or disgust on Dr. Gautier's face. Instead, he found the man staring at him sympathetically.

"That's quite a burden to have carried on your shoulders all these years. I imagine that it has always been at the back of your mind. And coming back here to Paris probably brought old memories to the surface."

"You don't look surprised." Hunter studied the doctor's kind face. "Did you somehow know even back then?"

Dr. Gautier shrugged. "I suspected there was more to the story of your dog running away from home. Your distress seemed disproportional."

He reached for the candy jar and stopped himself with an embarrassed smile.

"I suspected you felt guilty. But I didn't know what happened."

"I loved Coco so much. I don't even know what I hoped to find past the gate."

Dr. Gautier smiled slightly.

"Ah, it's the proverbial question in life. Don't we all seek greener pastures at some point in our lives, convinced that something wonderful lies just out of reach?"

The doctor reached for the candy jar again, stopped himself, and sat on his hands.

"Even with all your guilt, you must know that you meant no harm to come to your beloved pet."

"Intentions don't matter if something goes wrong." Hunter's voice was bitter.

"Ah, but I disagree," Dr. Gautier interjected. "The outcome was not set in stone. You acted foolishly, as all children are apt to do from time to time. But you did not act maliciously. There is a world of difference between the two."

Hunter listened to the words of the kind doctor, but he still felt angry at his younger self. Yet, he found himself agreeing to another visit later that week. He left the building sadder than he entered it. But he also felt a smidgen of relief that someone else finally knew his horrible secret.

He wasn't convinced that Dr. Gautier could help him with his control issues, but he was determined to make an effort. One thing was for certain. He didn't want to risk losing Amber. He had pushed Coco away that terrible day. He didn't want to make the same mistake with the woman of his dreams.

Chapter 24

Amber hunched over the workbench, happily cutting shards of glass for her first design. Three other students worked in close quarters as Monsieur Renaud walked among them, quietly offering advice and encouragement. Lately, this was where she felt happiest.

While work was as interesting as ever, Hunter's mom was a constant reminder of what Amber was missing when she returned home in the evenings. The art class was a balm to her wounds. Even three weeks after their breakup, she missed Hunter so much that she physically ached. At least in this warm, friendly class she could escape her thoughts for a few hours. That was what art did for her.

After class, Amber lingered, unwilling to go home. She was still there when Monsieur Renaud's wife came by on her way home from the University where she taught Literature.

"This must be the darling Amber!" she exclaimed, upon walking in the door. "My husband tells me what a sweet young woman you are!"

Amber blushed as the pretty, plump woman kissed her on both cheeks and then enveloped her in an enormous hug.

"It's a pleasure to meet you, Madame Renaud," she mumbled shyly.

"Ah, but you are so thin. You are not eating properly, my dear. You must come to dinner tonight at our home," she insisted, waving her hands in excitement.

"I don't want to be an imposition," Amber tried to say but Madame Renaud had already made up her mind and was consulting with her husband as to what wine they should serve.

Madame Renaud was like a whirlwind, arms and hands moving animatedly as she rattled on about what a lovely evening it would be and how she was going right away to purchase a bottle of wine.

"Oh, we do far too little entertaining!" she exclaimed, her face beaming.

Finally, she kissed her husband warmly and rushed out of the gallery.

"My wife gets quite excited, as you can see," Monsieur Renaud said with a smile.

Amber laughed. "I suppose I don't have much of a choice about dinner. I do hope that you don't mind."

"Mind? I'm delighted, my dear," Monsieur Renaud replied. "I should tell you that my wife and I are childless, but not by choice. My darling wife always wanted a daughter. You will make her so happy if you allow her to fuss over you like a mother hen tonight."

Amber had confided a little bit about her own childhood to Monsieur, leaving out a lot of details. He knew that she was essentially without parents of her own, but that Hunter's parents had showered her with affection.

Amber smiled shyly. "I suppose I'm not adverse to having a mother hen for the evening."

Secretly, she was relieved not to have to spend another evening by herself. She had spent a few more nights out with Hunter's mom, but that was bittersweet. She loved Mrs. Webb but, again, she was a constant reminder that Amber was going home to an empty hotel room.

Twenty minutes later, Madame Renaud returned, triumphantly waving a bottle of wine in one hand and clutching a handful of fresh flowers in the other. She whirled through the shop, leading the way up a dimly lit staircase to a cozy apartment.

Amber was almost embarrassed at living in such luxury all by herself when the Renauds were squeezed into such a tiny apartment. The couple's entire living space could have fit easily into her hotel suite with room to spare. But she had to admit that each inch of space was utilized. The stained glass windows, in particular, lit from behind with tiny Christmas tree lights on the small balcony, were beautiful works of art.

"Did you do these yourself?" she asked Monsieur Renaud, peering at them in awe.

"Indeed he did, dearest." Madame Renaud handed Amber a glass of wine. "My husband is ever so talented. One of the many reasons I fell in love with him."

"My wife overestimates my gifts," Monsieur Renaud said modestly. "But, yes, those are some of my first pieces many years ago."

"I don't know why I've never really appreciated stained glass art before now."

Amber admired the brilliance of the colors of each fractured piece of glass.

"It's amazing how an artist can take something that is broken and make it far more beautiful than the original piece," Madame Renaud said, peering over her shoulder.

"I think that it is a good analogy to life. If we have the right attitude, we can take the broken bits of our experiences and make ourselves stronger, more beautiful even."

"Huh," said Amber a bit skeptically.

She wasn't so sure about that right now. Since breaking up with Hunter, she felt like she was broken up into hundreds of pieces. Each piece was sharp and still painful.

"Ah! But in the midst of young love, it is hard to see the complete picture."

Monsieur Renaud indicated that Amber should make herself comfortable on the small sofa.

"I'm not sure that my broken relationship can be repaired."

She had confessed to Monsieur Renaud that the young man paying for her courses was her ex boyfriend.

"What is this? A lover's spat? What a tragedy for such a beautiful young woman!"

Madame Renaud leaned forward eagerly, her eyes misting.

"Now, darling, I'm not sure that Amber wants to discuss her love difficulties."

Monsieur Renaud squeezed his wife's hand.

Amber couldn't help it. She laughed at the absurdity of the woman's fascination.

"I'm afraid that my wife is obsessed with romance."

Monsieur Renaud smiled ruefully.

"I think that reading all of those romantic works for a living has seeped into her very blood."

"The greatest poets affect me deeply."

Madame Renaud sighed dramatically.

"I have such a wonderful love that I want to share it with the world."

"Perhaps we should offer Amber an appetizer, darling," Monsieur Renaud suggested, saving Amber at last.

"Oh, yes! I'm being a horrible host!"

Madame Renaud leaped up and hurried to the kitchen.

"Thanks," Amber whispered.

"She means well."

Monsieur Renaud sat in a small leather chair across from her. In the room's soft lighting he looked much younger than his actual age. Or perhaps simply being around his wife made him seem that way. In spite of their age, the couple acted like two people newly in love.

"She's just a hopeless romantic. Be careful or she'll try to set you up with one of her students at the University."

Amber grinned wryly. "I'm not ready now, but I might accept her offer in the future."

Monsieur Renaud considered her for a moment.

"Forgive an old man for being a hopeless romantic like his wife. But is there really no hope for reconciliation with the young man?"

Amber's eyes stung. She blinked back tears.

"We do love each other intensely. I don't doubt his love for me at all. If anything, it is that he smothers me."

"Ah!" Monsieur Renaud took a sip of his wine and then placed the glass carefully on the small coffee table.

"Do you think it strange that he should offer to pay for my courses?" Amber asked suddenly.

Monsieur Renaud shrugged his shoulders.

"Have any of our great artists been successful without a patron, my dear? The life of an artist usually means little pay. It is a blessing for an artist to have someone support them financially. Why should it be wrong if your patron is someone who loves you as well?"

Huh! A patron. That was worth thinking about further. Is that how Hunter saw himself?

Monsieur Renaud shifted in his seat.

"I can't tell you what to do about your young man, Amber. Only your heart knows the answer to that. But when I was starting out as an artist in this profession, my wife was the one who supported us while I got my training. It was her money that afforded me the shop and us this home."

Madame Renaud rejoined them, suggesting that they move to the table. The conversation turned to more generic topics.

A half hour later, Amber was enjoying the first course, a small plate of figs wrapped in bacon. She could scarcely believe that many families routinely gathered for evening meals lasting two to three hours.

As the evening wore on, she was treated to breaded pork chops with stewed chestnuts as the main course followed by a selection of cheeses served with salted apple slices. Finally, there was more wine with three squares of dark chocolate. By the time they were finished eating, it was nearly ten o'clock. Amber was glad that she had arranged for the driver to leave for his own evening meal and that he would be picking her up within the next half hour.

Although she had a wonderful evening, she was starting to feel the effects of her sleepless night the previous evening. Actually, she hadn't slept well since the breakup with Hunter.

"The meal was wonderful," she gushed as the Renauds walked with her downstairs to wait for the driver. "And both of you have been so kind."

"The pleasure was all ours, dear," Monsieur Renaud insisted. "Look at how happy you've made my wife."

Indeed, Madame Renaud was beaming like a small child.

"Please do agree to dine with us again," she insisted. "It does us good to have young people around."

"I could hardly object to being fed, could I?" Amber teased as she hugged each of the Renauds before meeting the driver.

Climbing into the car, she sank against the seat. She was happy but exhausted.

"I take it you had a pleasant evening, Mademoiselle?"

"Yes, Pierre," Amber replied, wishing that the driver would call her by her first name.

After she reached home, Amber thought to check her phone. Not that she was expecting anything. Hunter was being good about not contacting her too often. She got a text every now and then simply saying that he was thinking about her but that he didn't want to intrude on her space.

Over time, though, she craved intrusion. His controlling attitude seemed more and more like a small price to pay considering the constant heartache she felt without him.

You must be cracking up. Now you are missing some of his control freak tendencies.

She hadn't realized how much she had relied on Hunter before.

Turning on the phone, she grinned. She had two new text messages. Both from Hunter.

Chapter 25

Hunter felt a bit nauseous as the driver turned down the long, winding driveway leading to the old farmhouse that had belonged to his grandparents. This was his property now, bequeathed to him when his grandmother passed away. Gravel churned beneath the car's wheels and pinged the underside of the car. The sound took Hunter back in time.

This was his first visit since his grandmother had passed away and he felt assaulted by hundreds of memories all at once. As images of his beloved puppy sprang to mind, he had to swallow hard. He was grateful his mother had insisted on having a driver bring him. Otherwise, he might have stopped and turned the car back around.

Budding trees flanked the winding drive. An early spring was on its way to the countryside. Dr. Gautier was right, Hunter realized. In spite of the guilt, he also felt a small thrill to be back at last to a place that had given him so much joy in his childhood. He stared hard at the passing trees, remembering how his excitement would always be building at just this moment. In seconds he would glimpse the old farmhouse.

When the car rounded the final bend, they came upon the old metal privacy gate. Pierre got out, unlocked the padlock, and swung the gate open. After only a few more minutes, they arrived at the front of the old house.

Hunter admired its simple but sturdy construction. At one point in Hunter's family's history, this house had been a summer retreat rather than a year round home. As such, it lacked the grandeur of his parent's city apartment.

"Sir? Are you okay?"

Hunter looked up. The driver had already opened his door and was waiting for him to exit.

"Yes. Thanks, Pierre," he responded, thrusting his legs out of the car. "I hope you've brought a book to read. I might be awhile."

"Take your time, sir." Pierre smiled and nodded to a novel in the front seat of the car.

"And I thought you agreed to stop calling me sir."

Pierre laughed. "Yes, Hunter, sir."

Shaking his head, Hunter felt in his pockets for the house key. He expected the door to stick, but then remembered that the caretakers came by every few weeks to clean and maintain the property.

The door opened without a fuss and he walked inside, disappointed that the house no longer smelled like fresh baked bread. Now there was only a light scent of furniture polish.

As he walked through the modest home, he found comfort in the familiar furniture. There was his grandfather's leather recliner in one corner. His grandmother's sewing basket perched beside a comfortable chair. She had loved to sit by the fire and quilt on long winter days.

Hunter stooped in one corner and opened a small door. Beneath the staircase an old family member had installed a tiny child's play room. Peeking inside, he saw several of his old toys and a few books. Smiling, he remembered curling up on pillows inside with his puppy.

Then he bit his lip as that other memory crowded his head. Dr. Gautier had promised that the more he faced the one bad memory, the more he would be able to enjoy the pleasant memories.

Hunter hoped that was true. Backing away on his knees, he rose and walked through the rest of the home. He found everything clean and tidy.

The kitchen seemed quaint compared to modern standards, but the old giant stove stirred happy memories of his grandmother. He had probably been more of a hindrance than a help, but she had patiently allowed him to peel vegetables and mix ingredients in the large silver bowl that still sat on the kitchen counter. Hunter ran his fingers over everything.

Finally, he ventured upstairs, aware that he was procrastinating. After exploring all the other bedrooms, he paused at his childhood room. Taking a deep breath, he opened the door and walked inside.

The first thing he noticed was how small it seemed. He sat on the twin bed, running his fingers along the quilted surface. His grandmother had carefully pieced together several different wild animal fabrics. Every night he had gone to sleep covered in lions, tigers, bears, elephants, giraffes and chimpanzees. The walls were painted a pale blue. Faded yellow curtains stretched above the wide window that looked out across the great expanse of lawn.

Other than the bed, the only other furniture in the room was a small bureau, a wide bookcase packed with children's works, and an antique wooden rocking chair with a quilted cushion tied to the seat. One round rug covered a large part of the bare, polished wood floor. Just like the rest of the house, all the furnishings were clean and free of dust. The caretakers had done an excellent job of maintaining everything all these years.

Hunter stretched out on the bed and allowed himself to relive those moments of waking up to a wet tongue on his face in the mornings. Even now, he recalled the warmth of Coco's little body pressed against his chest while they slept. The feeling was bittersweet but not painful. A good sign, he thought. Maybe Dr. Gautier was right about him coming here.

Then again, Hunter still had the most painful exercise left. Dr. Gautier wanted him to retrace his steps. He was to experience that day as an adult observing his younger self that fateful day so many years ago. Perhaps that was why he was lying down, growing drowsier by the minute. If he allowed himself to fall asleep, he could avoid the next step.

But Amber's image flashed in his mind. The ache of missing her was too much. Sitting up, he swung his legs off the bed and marched resolutely downstairs. He stopped by the kitchen, his mind conjuring up breakfast with his grandparents. Then he moved outside, forcing himself to remain detached as he imagined younger Hunter racing across the yard with Coco.

One day during a therapy session, Dr. Gautier had taken a measuring stick and showed Hunter how tall he had been when he first met him. Hunter had been taken aback by how small he was back then. For the first time, he had been able to truly see that younger version of himself as a child. Now, he made himself picture how small this young boy was running to the gate.

Older now, he watched with new eyes the curiosity and excitement in the little boy's face as he approached the gate. For the first time since that day, he allowed himself to remember that he had planned on stopping by a small shop that sold sausages in the nearby village. He had imagined how happy Coco would be sitting by his feet and gobbling up such a wonderful treat. He had planned to take Coco to the small duck pond in the park. Young Hunter had wanted to see Coco's excitement at seeing all those ducks.

Hunter stopped suddenly. He was at the old wooden gate. Fully grown, he had no trouble seeing right over the top of the low gate. But he realized that his younger self would have been too short to see over. His younger self strained to reach the latch.

Hunter reached up to open the actual gate as it now existed. The rusted latch flaked in his hand. As the gate swung open, it whined. Swallowing hard, Hunter gazed out. Not much had changed over the years except that the small dirt road was much narrower than he remembered.

Remembering Dr. Gautier's instructions, Hunter forced himself to witness his memories as an objective observer. He watched the little boy drop down and beg the dog to come with him. The little dog looked up quizzically. The boy began shouting about sausages just around the corner. As Hunter the adult watched in sick fascination, the child raised a small booted foot and shoved the dog.

The startled dog squealed and backed away. Then he trotted briskly down the small road. The little boy yelled the dog's name. He trotted after the puppy. But the dog was much faster and disappeared around the corner.

Hunter forced himself to walk down to where the road forked. Even today, it looked barren. Hunter allowed himself to remember how frightened he had been. And then he realized that the five-year-old version of himself had simply been too scared to go down that road alone. As a grownup, Hunter watched that little kid stare down the road. He felt sorry for him.

Hunter turned and walked back to the gate because that was what his younger version had done that day. Little Hunter had sat by the gate sobbing until his grandparents found him. Looking back, Hunter realized that his grandparents must have guessed what had happened. How else would the gate have gotten open? And yet, they had done nothing but hug him and search the road for hours.

How was it that he remembered that part now but had somehow blocked it out as a child? Had it been simple shame? Shame at having kicked his dog and then being too afraid to track him down on his own. He now remembered that he had been afraid to leave the gate, convinced that Coco would come back to find him.

As Hunter's thoughts returned to the present day, he sat in the waning sunlight, staring off into the distance. As he did, he was startled to see a flash of color moving toward him. For a split second, he thought that Coco had been resurrected and was coming back.

He squinted and just made out a bicyclist. Hunter got to his feet and brushed off his pants. As the bicyclist got closer, he had to blink a few times. He was really hallucinating now. The rider looked so much like Amber that he actually took a step back in shock.

Chapter 26

Amber wasn't sure why she was riding a bicycle down a lonely country road. In fact, the rational part of her brain told her that this was sheer nonsense, that she just had to concentrate more on getting over Hunter. Perhaps she should have allowed Madame Renaud to set her up on a date with one of her students. There was even a hot guy in her stained-glass art class that kept trying to get her attention.

But nobody else seemed remotely interesting compared to Hunter. Even the hot guy fell short of her expectations. Would she ever be attracted to someone as much as Hunter? In the end, her desire to see if she and Hunter still had a connection, if there was still that electricity between them after all these weeks apart, was what drove her to take a local train to the small village near Hunter's home in the country. Armed with a hand drawn map, she had rented a bicycle and set out down a lonely road.

Part of her expected to cycle all the way there, come upon a locked gate, and have to return right back to the train station. There was one final train headed back to the city later that evening and she fully planned on being on it. What were the odds that Hunter would still be there? She knew that he had selected today for his visit. Mrs. Webb had casually mentioned the fact the day before. She had also explained that she wouldn't be needing Amber for the day.

As Amber pedaled down the road, she grinned to herself. As much as the Webbs were making Hunter avoid pestering her, they had been dropping more than subtle hints that they hoped that she would give their son another chance. Well, this was more than a subtle hint, she thought with a giggle. Too bad this was probably not going to work. It wasn't like Hunter was going to be waiting for her to turn the corner.

Spotting another fork in the road, Amber stopped and consulted Mrs. Webb's small map. She needed to take a right at this corner and then follow the road until she reached the first gate. Mrs. Webb had insisted that it would probably be open. Feeling a bit foolish, Amber started pedaling again. As she made her way down the path, she saw someone sitting off to the side, leaning against a fence.

Her rational mind smirked.

There he is, just sitting there waiting for you. Yeah, right!

She pedaled closer and saw that it was a guy. He stood and brushed the dirt from his trousers.

The sun must be getting to me. That looks exactly like Hunter.

Yes, Hunter was supposed to be on the property today. But surely he wouldn't just be sitting there staring down the road. Had the Webbs tipped him off?

She got closer and realized that it was Hunter. She stopped several feet away when she saw his mouth hanging open.

He looked as pale as though he had seen a ghost. Okay, so the Webbs had definitely not mentioned she might be dropping by.

"Hunter, are you okay?"

Hunter wobbled on his feet.

"You're not a vision?" he whispered. "This is real?"

Amber hopped off the bike, letting it fall beside her. She hurried to his side and wrapped her arms around his waist.

"It's really me, Hunter. Are you sick?"

Hunter leaned against her and she had to brace her feet to hold him upright. But then he steadied himself and lightly stroked her cheek.

"I've been having flashbacks all day," he murmured. "And now you show up just when I need you the most."

Amber looked into his eyes, those gorgeous green gems that now glistened with tears. With a shock, she realized how much he clearly needed her. She was suddenly the strong one. Or maybe she had been strong all along? Was that possible? Had her insecurities blinded her to her own strengths?

As they stared at each other, Amber felt electricity building between them. Whatever their issues, she knew without a doubt that she and Hunter needed each other. If fate was a real thing, then perhaps they were even meant to be together.

"I love you, Hunter Webb," she said, her voice breathless. "We may end up driving each other insane, but I can't live without you."

"I hope this isn't a hallucination," Hunter muttered.

Tilting her head up, Amber found his lips with her own, tugging gently until she heard him groan. She broke away with a small sigh.

Hunter smiled. "So you're giving me another chance?"

"I know you've worked so hard in therapy. I would never forgive myself if I didn't at least try to make things work between us."

"You don't know how happy that makes me."

Hunter cradled her face and leaned down to kiss her softly.

Amber felt the rightness of the kiss as she sank against him.

"Bring the bike and follow me," Hunter said, breaking away. "Or would you rather I took it for you?"

He seemed so hesitant that Amber laughed.

"I think I can manage. But thanks for asking and not assuming what I wanted."

As they approached the old farmhouse, Hunter seemed nervous.

"I know the place is probably not the estate you were expecting."

But Amber was spellbound.

"It's lovely. Exactly what I imagined an old farmhouse in the countryside to look like."

Seeing the car, Amber glanced at Hunter. "Did you drive here on your own?"

Hunter followed her gaze. "No. Pierre must have fallen asleep in the front seat."

"Then let's try not to wake him," Amber said in a whisper.

Hunter grinned as he tiptoed up the front porch steps. He opened the door and motioned her inside.

"After you, Mademoiselle."

"It's wonderful. Cozy and romantic. The kind of place you could raise a family," Amber said before thinking.

She flushed. "I mean, the kind of place that anyone would be happy raising a family," she sputtered.

But Hunter only smiled and led her inside.

"What about the kitchen? Should I have someone come in to replace the appliances?"

Amber considered. "Only if they could keep the integrity of the house. Like how your parents arranged their kitchen.

I bet the stove still works. And those butcher block counters could just be sanded down."

Hunter nodded his head.

"Would you help with the design?" he asked, coming close to nuzzle her neck.

"I think I could arrange that."

Amber tried to keep her voice light. She suddenly wondered if things were moving too quickly.

"Is the bathroom in working order?"

Hunter released her. "Right around the corner."

When she stepped back into the hallway, she didn't see Hunter at first. Then he stepped in from the porch.

"Would you like to see the upstairs?"

"Of course!"

Amber loved the quaint rooms with the antique furniture.

"What a charming child's room."

She stepped into Hunter's old bedroom and tried to imagine him as the little boy with the puppy. But she wouldn't bring that subject up now.

"That bike ride made me hungry. Shall we wake up Pierre and find a place to get dinner?"

"Already taken care of," Hunter said, his voice cautious.

"Why, Mr. Webb. Are your control freak tendencies appearing again?"

Amber saw him cringe and punched his shoulder lightly.

"If so, I would like to commend you for the excellent timing."

Hunter looked visibly relieved.

"So it's okay to be a control freak from time to time?"

"Like all things, there is a time and a place for your control freak tendencies."

Amber followed him down the stairs and through the living room.

She was starting to believe that she and Hunter might have a chance at happily ever after.

Chapter 27

Kayla Ross strode out of the court room with her head high and her sunglasses firmly in place. Fortunately, the press had disappeared almost completely once it became apparent that most of the trial was happening without glimpses of the famous Webb family. She supposed she should be grateful for that.

But of course she wasn't. She was furious.

True, a lot of her anger was focused on her stupid parents for getting the family into this mess. Gone. Everything. Bank accounts seized while the courts decided what was owed to the Webb family. Her mother's grim-faced attorney had explained that only Kayla's personal bank account could be accessed now.

Kayla couldn't even stay in Paris. The family home turned out to be a rental. She had only days to vacate. The expensive furnishings her mother had insisted on had already been removed to be auctioned. Kayla had been sleeping on an inflatable mattress for nearly a week.

As she hurried to the car, Kayla's high heels clicked against the concrete floor of the basement garage. The sound echoed menacingly.

Kayla's hands trembled as she opened the door and slid inside the cheap rental car. Her parents were facing at least a year of imprisonment for stealing trade secrets and selling them to the Webb family's rival competitors. More distressing for Kayla, though, were the stiff fines and exorbitant penalties that had brought her family to financial ruin.

But Kayla wasn't thinking of her parent's criminal activities at the moment. She was thinking about a certain blonde who had swept Hunter Webb off his feet and ruined any chance that Kayla herself might have had with him.

"You little witch!" Kayla roared, slapping the steering wheel in frustration.

So much of this could have been avoided if Kayla was the one on Hunter's arm. Her father might have been elevated in the company. Her mother . . . Well, perhaps even her mother wouldn't have gone off the deep end. The woman had always had problems. But she had grown desperate the last year.

For a second, Kayla wondered what exactly her mother had done to lose so much money that she had been driven to theft. Did she have a gambling habit Kayla and her father were not aware of? Kayla sighed. It didn't really matter at this point. What little money remained would soon be gone.

And what was she supposed to do? Go out and get a job like some common nothing. Kayla refused to lower herself like the blonde witch. Was she supposed to hope some rich guy was going to discover her ringing up groceries like a poor person? No, she would find a way to make Hunter and that little witch pay.

Wiping away a few tears, Kayla started the car and backed up. She would pack up her nicest clothes and take the cheapest flight she could get back to the States. At least there she had her parents' house to live in while she figured out what to do. She could only hope that the courts didn't try to seize that property as well.

While she drove, Kayla schemed about how to get her revenge. Everybody, even Hunter's precious Amber Holloway, had dark places in their past. Kayla was going to make sure that the perfect Hunter and his little witch girlfriend were going to have their happy ever after ruined.

Chapter 28

Hunter smiled as he woke up. Just knowing that Amber was in the next room made him happy. He could scarcely believe that he now had her back in his life. He was determined never to risk losing her again. He had elaborate plans to propose to her.

Slipping quietly out of bed, he crept to the bathroom and softly shut the door. He showered quickly, trying to stay quiet. When he opened the door to peek in her room, Amber was still sound asleep. That wasn't too surprising since it was just a little past five o'clock in the morning.

Hunter wrote Amber a note and propped it against the kettle. She wouldn't go anywhere without her first cup of morning tea.

Softly closing the hotel suite door, he hurried to the elevator and impatiently waited for it to come to their floor. An elderly woman from down the hall was taking her miniature poodle for a walk and the dog sniffed at Hunter's shoes.

"Good morning," Hunter said politely. But he was too distracted for small talk this morning.

After allowing the woman and her dog to exit first, Hunter hurried through the lobby and out the grand front doors of the luxury hotel.

Pierre was already waiting with the car when Hunter, hunching his shoulders against a brisk wind, arrived outside. Although spring had arrived, the weather was still quite cool, particularly in the early morning hours.

Pierre grinned as Hunter slid into the car.

"Going to be a beautiful day."

Pierre eyed Hunter in the rear view mirror before easing the car into traffic.

"Thanks again for arranging such an early appointment with your uncle."

Pierre shrugged as he navigated the car into an older, much quieter, part of the city.

"Uncle Gustav doesn't sleep much since Aunt Genevieve died a few years ago."

Hunter didn't know what to say to that. Fortunately, Pierre seemed content to drive in silence.

In spite of his excitement, Hunter felt his eyes closing in the warmth of the car. He jerked awake as the car came to a stop. Blinking his eyes open and stretching, he saw that they had arrived in a section devoid of modern buildings. This was a quiet, tree-lined street with sedate architecture. New leaf buds and flowers helped create the illusion that he had been transported back in time. Looking around, Hunter recognized an expensive tailor shop where his father had all of his suits made to order.

Pierre opened the door and Hunter stepped out, feeling awkward for a moment because Pierre was doing this favor as a friend rather than his hired driver. But Pierre seemed unperturbed as he lifted a hand to indicate the building that they would be entering.

The two men walked past the tailor's shop and a bakery where sweet smells wafted from inside. Pierre paused at the door to a small jewelry shop. Although there was nothing extravagant about the entrance, Hunter knew that some of the finest and most expensive jewelry were fashioned inside.

Pierre unlocked the door and Hunter followed him inside. After securing the door and resetting an alarm, Pierre pointed to a narrow flight of stairs at the back of the shop.

"Sorry, there's no elevator." He mounted the first step.

"I've tried to get him to move into a more modern building or least swap apartments with one of his tenants. But he's stubborn as a mule."

Hunter eyed the stairs above them.

"What floor does he live on?"

"The top," Pierre called back, quickly climbing the steps. "Might want to save your breath."

The top turned out to be the fifth floor. Hunter was quite surprised. Buildings of this period were built with the smallest units on the top during an era when it was common to house servants. The second floors were generally occupied by those who owned the shops on the first floors. The rationale was that the second floor was more removed from street noises but had fewer steps to climb - a bonus since elevators were not installed in these older buildings.

"I'm surprised your Uncle never considered renovating the building to include an elevator."

Hunter was panting. He felt a dribble of sweat running down his neck.

"I mention getting an elevator every time I see him. But he says that the stairs keep him young."

Pierre had managed to arrive at the top looking fresh.

Hunter took out his handkerchief and dried his face. Maybe he needed a gym membership.

"He must be quite spry. I can't imagine bringing groceries up all this way."

Pierre sighed and shook his head.

"I suspect it is more about his memories of when he and my Aunt were first married. They could only afford the top floor. After he became renown for his work, he was able to eventually buy out all the other owners and rent the apartments. By that time, though, Aunt Genevieve refused to move."

He laughed. "She didn't want an elevator either."

Pierre knocked on an ornate door.

They didn't have long to wait. The door opened to reveal a slender, smiling gentleman with wispy tufts of white hair that stuck up on his head in Albert Einstein fashion. Monsieur Benoit was dressed in a dark pin-striped suit with a red silk tie. The suit, though made of fine materials, was obviously at least a few decades old. However, the cut of the jacket fit his body perfectly.

"Good morning, Pierre," he said in a pleasant French voice.

"Good morning, Uncle. May I present Hunter Webb. Hunter, this is my Uncle Gustav."

"I am looking forward to doing business with you, Monsieur Webb."

Gustav extended a hand and Hunter was surprised at the firmness of the elderly man's grip.

"It's a pleasure to meet you, Monsieur Benoit," Hunter replied in French. "I am honored that you are willing to design and craft a ring for me. I know that you are in high demand."

"Pierre has told me a little bit about your lovely young lady." Gustav winked. "My favorite projects involve matters of the heart."

He turned and pushed the door open wide.

"Please come in and make yourselves comfortable."

Hunter was astonished at how small the apartment was in comparison to the famous jeweler's wealth and status. The square footage made the hotel suite he shared with Amber seem palatial.

Gustav led them into the tiny kitchen. Though small, the room benefited from modern appliances and a beautiful window that looked out over the neighborhood. A small round table held a tray of croissants, fresh fruit, and an ornate silver pot of coffee.

Once satisfied that everyone had partaken of the light breakfast, Gustav led them to the living room. Here, a sofa and a few comfortable chairs surrounded a polished coffee table.

"Have a seat while I fetch my sketchbook."

Hunter chose a winged-back leather chair while Pierre sat down on a paisley overstuffed chair.

"I assume that is your Aunt Genevieve." Hunter pointed at an ornately framed painting of a beautiful woman.

Pierre smiled. "Yes. Uncle Gustav had it commissioned for their twentieth wedding anniversary. I believe she was in her early forties when it was done."

Hunter stood to admire the brush strokes. The style looked familiar. Leaning closer, he saw the signature and whistled. The artist was a well-known recluse who did not do private paintings.

"They've been friends since grade school," Pierre said when Hunter gave him a questioning look.

"He did this portrait as a favor."

Hunter wanted to ask more questions, but Gustav reappeared with a thick sketch pad.

"As an artist, I am guessing that you have ideas already," Gustav said, smiling graciously.

Hunter felt as though the man was studying him keenly. He grinned.

"But of course. But primarily just the materials that I want to use. I'm anxious to see what you come up with."

"And what stones were you thinking of? Diamonds or another jewel entirely?"

"I was hoping that you could do something with an emerald. Amber, my girlfriend, says that my eyes are like jewels. So I thought it might be a clever idea for an engagement ring. Actually, I'm hoping to incorporate emeralds into the wedding rings as well."

Hunter flushed.

"Assuming that she agrees to marry me."

Hunter added a small nervous smile. He had a sudden horror of having the ring made only to have Amber refuse to marry him.

"Ah, but Pierre tells me that your love is very real. Very passionate."

Gustav looked over at his nephew and winked.

Hunter glanced over at his driver.

Pierre ducked his head.

"I just told him that you seemed very much in love," he said, looking nervous.

Hunter laughed, shaking off his fears.

"I suppose that you've seen quite a bit as our driver," he admitted.

Pierre looked relieved.

"Please believe me when I say I don't make it a habit to speak about my clients."

Hunter waved a hand to dismiss the driver's concerns.

"Don't worry, Pierre. I know that you've been discrete."

"About that emerald?" Gustav interrupted gently.

Hunter swung his attention back to the elderly gentleman.

"Yes, of course. I would like the most beautiful gem you can get your hands on. Money is no object. However, I prefer quality to mere size."

"I understand," Gustav said thoughtfully. "I have seen a few that might be of interest to you. But first let me know what sort of setting you have in mind."

"Modern and elegant. And I prefer silver to gold."

"What about platinum?"

Hunter shook his head.

"I know that it is more valuable than silver or gold. But my parents have silver rings."

He broke off and shrugged.

"My parents have had such a wonderful marriage. I'm hoping that silver rings will bring us marital good fortune."

Hunter thought that Gustav would find his reasoning foolish. But he was pleasantly surprised.

"Ah, there is nothing wrong with having sentimental reasons for your choices. It shows that you care more for what the rings mean than simply how much money that you can spend."

Gustav leaned back in his chair and smiled.

"As it happens, I have a particular fondness for silver myself."

He held out his hand so that Hunter could see his own wedding band.

"Even now I find that this ring gives me comfort. I only hope that you can find a small fraction of the happiness that I found with my own departed wife."

"You must have loved her dearly," Hunter said softly.

Gustav smiled. "Yes, I did. However, the neighbors probably wondered about our relationship from time to time. My dear Genevieve had a fiery temper."

Gustav tapped his chin thoughtfully.

"I suppose I was rather headstrong in my own way as well. But we loved each other just as passionately as we sometimes argued."

Pierre stood and made his way to the kitchen. He retrieved the silver coffee pot and refilled everyone's cups.

"I remember that you always found a way to make Aunt Genevieve laugh when she got angry."

Gustav smiled. After taking a small sip of fresh coffee, he carefully placed his cup and saucer on the table.

"Ah, that's one of the secrets to being happily married. Laughter can resolve a multitude of disagreements."

Moving his sketch pad to a new position, Gustav picked up a pencil and began to draw.

Hunter watched, fascinated, as inspiration motivated Gustav's aged fingers. In a matter of minutes, he produced a drawing for inspection.

"It's perfect," Hunter said, thrilled at the simplicity of the design.

"I'll make a mock up with the stone I have in mind," Gustav said, apparently not surprised that Hunter liked the drawing immediately.

"How long do you think it will take?"

Hunter knew how popular the jeweler's services were.

"I'll contact my associate this afternoon. He travels extensively so it may take a week or so to get my hands on the stone. But in the meantime, I'll make a mock up with inexpensive materials. I should have something to show you within the next week."

"And once I approve the final design?" Hunter hoped he wasn't being too pushy.

Gustav smiled. "Ah, love is impatient, is it not?"

"I'm sorry," Hunter said hastily.

"It is refreshing! Don't worry. Once the design is approved with the stone, I will devote my full attention to the project until it is finished. I daresay that you could have the finished ring in hand within a month."

"That would be wonderful."

"I suppose you have a date for proposing to the young lady?"

Hunter grinned.

"I haven't planned a specific date yet. Please don't think that you have to rush. I mean, sure, I want to ask her sooner rather than later. But I want the ring to be perfect."

"I shall certainly do my best." Gustav pushed himself to his feet.

Hunter rose as well, aware of how much time he had already taken.

"Thanks again for agreeing to take me on as a client."

"It's my pleasure," Gustav shuffled to the door. "I'll contact you when the mock up ring is completed."

Hunter whistled as he and Pierre made their way back down the staircase. Now that he had taken this first step towards getting Amber to marry him, he felt as though he could float back down to the first floor.

Chapter 29

Flying coach was a new experience for Kayla. Her head ached from trying to figure out her current financial situation. Worse, the man crammed into the seat on her left smelled so bad that she thought she might literally become ill.

And they hadn't even finished boarding the plane yet! How on earth was she going to survive an entire trip with that foul odor?

"I've been training as a soldier in Israel," he told her politely as he sat down in his military fatigues.

Kayla gave him a withering glance and ignored him. But a few seconds later she got up to flag down a flight attendant.

"You have to move my seat," Kayla said when she got the woman's attention.

"I'm sorry, but this is a full flight."

The attendant tried to move around Kayla to assist a woman shoving an over-sized purse into the overhead bin.

"You don't understand. The man sitting next to me reeks so badly that I'm going to puke."

The attendant paused and glanced back toward the man in military fatigues.

"Look, I've already gotten a few complaints from other passengers. But there is literally nothing I can do. Every single seat on board, including first class, is taken. The only thing you can do is to take a later flight."

"Why not make him take the later flight?" Kayla demanded. "He's the one stinking up the place."

Another flight attendant appeared.

"Is there a problem?" he asked sternly.

"I was just explaining to this young lady that we can't change her seat because the plane is full."

"I paid a lot of money to take this flight. And now you're saying I have to sit beside someone who reeks so badly that other people have complained?"

The second attendant shrugged.

"He paid for his ticket same as you. Maybe book first class next time so this kind of thing is less likely to happen."

The first attendant tapped her watch.

"We're getting close to taking off. You'll have to either return to your seat or get off the plane."

Furious, Kayla stomped back to her seat and yanked her overnight bag from the bin above her head. The metal buckle from her bag swung down and clipped her cheek, causing her to wince. Great! She would probably have a bruise on top of everything else.

She wanted the military guy to look up so that she could say something nasty to him. Instead, he kept his head down and feigned sleep.

Curious glances followed her as the male attendant escorted her off the plane and back to the gate. Kayla wanted to scream at the passengers to mind their own business.

After waiting several minutes for the attendant at the desk to even acknowledge her, she discovered that her ordeal was not anywhere near being over.

"I'm sorry, but I'm the wrong person to help you," the woman explained. "I only do boardings and my shift is ending now. You'll have to call a customer service representative to help you reschedule."

"Thanks for nothing, then!" Kayla snatched her ticket and stalked down the terminal.

Her headache was totally out of control now. She felt as though someone was driving an ice pick into her right eye socket.

She stopped at the nearest shop and purchased aspirin, a soda, and a king-sized candy bar. After consuming all three, she finally called the airline.

"But I only got off the flight because it was physically impossible to sit next to that man," she insisted twenty minutes later.

She was aware that her voice had risen so loud that several people around her were staring.

"I can't believe that you are going to charge me a fee for something that your attendants should have handled better. Sitting in stench for an overnight flight is not reasonable."

After another fifteen minutes, with a manager called to the phone, Kayla had managed to prove that she normally flew first class and that she and her parents were platinum members. By a stroke of luck, she discovered she had enough points to upgrade her flight.

Perhaps fearing that her family would switch allegiance to a different airline, the manager finally apologized for the confusion and arranged for a complimentary stay at a local hotel until her flight the following morning. Kayla would have to get up at a ridiculous hour in the morning to make the flight. But at least now she would fly first class.

She hoped that this turn of events would mark a change in her luck.

Chapter 30

Amber walked along the busy street, grateful for the sunny skies and the warm weather. She was thrilled to be back in Paris after having spent several weeks back in the States getting a long-term visitor visa to extend her stay. Hunter had asked her to postpone her college classes and stay with him through the summer.

The first few days back had been rainy. Today, she was finally able to stroll around without lugging an umbrella. Simply feeling the sun on her face made Amber feel happy.

As grateful as she was to have the daily services of a chauffeur, sometimes Amber just wanted to walk around by herself, exploring the little streets that held inexpensive shops, bakeries, and cafes. She found that her French had progressed enough that she could finally understand much of what the locals said. Even when she struggled, the keepers of smaller shops didn't get frustrated and automatically switch to English.

She purchased a small bouquet of flowers for the hotel suite as well as a yummy fruit-filled pastry to enjoy as she strolled back. Hunter had gone out earlier that morning, but she was hoping that he would soon be back from his mysterious errand.

Hunter was acting strangely. Something was going on and she was concerned that he showed no interest in involving her.

Plus, she had been annoyed when their Saturday morning had been spoiled by the errand. After all, he hadn't seen her in weeks. Worse, he had acted jumpy. She didn't want to leap to any conclusions. But she felt uneasy.

She had just put the flowers in a vase when Hunter returned.

"Hey, Gorgeous. How was your morning?" Hunter kissed her lightly on the cheek.

"Great," she said, peering around to look for packages.

"I thought you were going shopping. Didn't you find what you were looking for?"

Hunter blinked rapidly.

"Did I say shopping? I meant that I was . . . um . . . going to look at some things," he said vaguely.

"Hunter, what is going on? I thought we agreed to stop keeping things from each other."

Amber didn't want an argument, but this new secrecy was starting to worry her.

Hunter sighed unexpectedly.

"Okay, I guess I should tell you. You know how I said that everyone leaves the city for the first of May?"

"Yes. You said that most of the shops and restaurants close because it's the Paris version of Labor Day. You mentioned we might spend the weekend at the house in the country."

Hunter rubbed his neck.

"Well, unfortunately I have some bad news. I had some contractors looking at the farmhouse. Turns out we have some plumbing issues. We won't be able to go there after all."

"Oh, well, it is an old home."

Amber tried to hide her disappointment. She had been looking forward to playing house.

Hunter bit his lip.

"I'm afraid that isn't the worst of it. Dad needs me to meet an important client in Texas."

"Texas? You're going to Texas? When? And for how long?" Amber couldn't keep the dismay from her voice.

Hunter held up his hand.

"Really, it won't be that bad. And you can come with me. The company booked us a decent hotel and the weather should be warmer than here. You can hang out by the pool while I'm in meetings."

"I suppose that's not so terrible. I wouldn't mind just relaxing by the pool, that's for sure."

She felt puzzled. Going on a business trip with Hunter was not the worst thing in the world, even if he did have to work. Was this why he was acting so weird? Or was there something that he still wasn't telling her?

She sighed. "I was just excited to spend the long weekend with you."

Hunter put his arms around her.

"I promise I'll make it up to you."

"So when do we leave?"

"I thought we could fly out the twenty-eighth to avoid some of the crowds leaving the city."

Amber gaped at him. She thought of her limited wardrobe here in Paris. With the exception of jeans, tee shirts, and sweaters, almost all of her clothing was for work.

"But that doesn't leave me much time for shopping. I'll need shorts, a swimsuit, maybe a dress, some sandals . . . "

She broke off, deep in thought.

"Maybe I should start looking today." She grabbed her purse.

"You're going shopping now?"

"Did you have something planned for this afternoon?

Hunter scrunched his face. "I'm supposed to meet with the contractors this afternoon."

He took her hand. "But why don't we get some lunch together first? Then you can shop while I go see what needs to be done at the farmhouse."

"Perfect! This works out better for both of us."

"Pizza or Chinese?" Hunter asked as they headed for the elevator.

"Pizza," Amber declared, suddenly excited about shopping for the unexpected trip.

An hour later, Amber bit into her own personal pizza. Called the Basquiat, it was topped with salami and figs. The Pink Flamingo restaurant wasn't fancy. In fact, it was occupied mostly by students. But the selection of pizzas were unique.

Hunter was more adventurous than she was, munching on a pizza with chicken and prawns prepared in green curry.

Surrounded by local students, Amber felt completely at ease. No need to worry about special forks or wearing the right clothes. She could just be herself.

"So what part of Texas are we going to?" Amber asked after polishing off her second slice.

Hunter pulled another slice of pizza off the pan and offered it to her first.

Amber shook her head. She wasn't exactly a fan of curry, green or not.

"What was that?" Hunter seemed distracted and took a large bite of pizza.

Amber shook her head. Hunter was obviously starving the way he was plowing through his food.

"I asked what part of Texas we were going to. So I can look up the area."

Hunter carefully chewed his food, taking his time, and following up with a long drink of beer.

"I'd have to look up the name again," he said vaguely.

Amber felt a little lump in her stomach. What on earth was going on?

Chapter 31

After some consideration, Kayla splurged on the car service to get home. She had no idea what a taxi might cost and she was just too tired after her flight to deal with the possibility of a chatty driver or a disgusting car. At least with the car service, the driver would only speak to her if she started a conversation.

Sinking into the leather seat, Kayla felt almost normal even with so little sleep. This was how her life was supposed to be. She had been reared to believe that other people would take care of her needs as well as anticipate what she might want. The driver was a regular who recognized her. He politely took her things and then kept his mouth shut for the entire drive. Exactly how she liked it.

The car was also stocked with drinks and snacks. She hungrily ate two candy bars, a bag of chips, and drank a soda. Although her jeans felt snug, she didn't particularly care at the moment. Gaining a pound or two was the least of her problems.

Once she got home, Kayla was elated that housekeeping had been by and that everything was clean and tidy. She took a long shower and ordered takeout from her favorite restaurant.

While she waited, she found a notebook and marker in her desk drawer and started a list of things to do.

Research the little witch's family

Contact bank about funds

Cancel school classes

Ruin reputation of the Webbs

After her food arrived, Kayla ate until her stomach ached and then collapsed into bed.

Chapter 32

The next week felt like torture. Hunter checked his phone all the time, hoping for a message from the jeweler. Worse, when he was around Amber, all Hunter could think about was how he was going to propose in less than a month.

He hadn't expected to feel so nervous. But suddenly he had doubts that she would agree to marry him. After all, not much time had lapsed since their breakup had finally ended. He was sure that she was going to think he was insane for rushing her to make a decision this quickly.

Even parental reassurances were not enough to keep him from worrying.

"Really, Hunter, I know that she loves you," his mother said to him over lunch one day.

"You've just got the jitters."

Hunter jabbed his chicken with his fork.

"But what if she thinks I'm still too much of a control freak?"

"Easy on the poultry," Mr. Webb said, putting a hand on Hunter's shoulder.

"Your mom is right. I was a nervous wreck before I proposed to her."

Mrs. Webb laughed. "I actually thought he was angry with me. He had nothing to say when we were on dates."

"Not helpful, mom," Hunter moaned. "That's happening already."

"I'm sorry, Hunter. I'm just trying to say that what you are going through is very natural."

Mrs. Webb patted his arm.

"Don't you have a big exhibition coming up at the gallery right before you leave for Texas?"

Mr. Webb paused with his steak knife raised in the air.

"Maybe you should volunteer to work extra hours. Keeping busy will help keep your mind off the proposal."

Hunter sat up straighter.

"That's a good idea. But do you think Amber would mind?"

"I'll make a point of having Amber over for dinner on the nights when you are working late."

Mrs. Webb placed a hand over her wine glass when the server tried to pour more.

"You know we love spending time with her. I'll arrange a day to go shopping as well."

Hunter felt a bit of his tension ease. His mom always knew just what to say to make him feel better. He returned to the art gallery feeling better. Staying busy with work would surely put his mind at ease.

Madame Lebas agreed to his plan at once.

"I was trying to give you more time with that young lady of yours. But I most certainly could use your helping in getting ready for the new exhibit."

As if a thought had just occurred to her, Madame Lebas put down the guest list she had been working on. She moved close enough that Hunter smelled a waft of her expensive perfume. Her voice softened.

"Is everything okay, darling? Have you and Amber had a quarrel?"

Hunter sighed. "No, but I've been on edge. The thing is . . ."

Madame Lebas tilted her head and waited for him to continue.

"Well, I am planning to propose to her at the end of the month."

Madame Lebas smiled broadly. She nodded her head sagely.

"Ah! Now it all makes sense!"

"What makes sense?" Hunter asked in confusion.

Madame Lebas grinned. When she shook her head, her dangling jade earrings swayed.

"Your distraction this past week. Silly little things. Like you said you were going to go pick up a client and you walked into the supply closet. And I found the key to the front door in the refrigerator this morning."

Hunter felt the blood rushing to his face. He was not the type of guy to go walking around like an airhead.

But Madame Lebas simply smiled.

"Don't be embarrassed, my dear boy. Love makes us do strange things. I'm just glad that things are going so well for you."

"But I feel so miserable. I'm tongue tied when I'm around her. I know I've been ignoring her."

Madame Lebas made a clucking sound with her tongue.

"We must figure out a way to show Amber that your feelings are just as powerful as before."

"But what can I do?"

Hunter knew he probably sounded petulant and childish. He certainly felt pathetic.

"You must call her right now. Yes, even while she is at work. Tell her that she has been on your mind all day. You want her to ask for a day off next week to see the Luxembourg gardens. And then you will pick the sunniest and warmest day to take her."

"But what about the exhibit?"

Madame Lebas laughed.

"Oh, I will certainly keep you busy before your little day trip. But you will be able to focus on your duties more if you are not walking around in a fog. Amber will be flattered that you are willing to take time off from work to take her. Most importantly, it will give her something to look forward to on evenings when you are here working late."

She winked. "A winning situation for everyone. Including me!"

Hunter grinned. "I suppose that could work. I'm sure I can convince her boss to let her off for a day."

The gallery phone began to ring and Madame Lebas reached out to get it before Hunter could answer it himself.

"Get busy and make that phone call," she said to him quickly, her expression turning serious. "We have an exhibit to prepare for."

Hunter ducked into an empty room and pulled out his cell phone.

"Hey, Gorgeous. How's work going?"

"Hi, Hunter. Is anything wrong?"

"No, not at all," Hunter replied. "I've just been thinking about you all day. I can't keep you out of my mind."

Hunter heard a little catch in her voice as she responded.

"Oh, how sweet! But, Hunter, I'm in a meeting with your mother."

"Tell mom I'm terribly sorry, but I need to speak to you. Can you ask to step away for a moment?"

"Um . . . Sure," Amber responded in a puzzled voice.

Amber must have lowered the phone. Her voice sounded faint as she spoke to his mom.

"Give me a second, Hunter," she said, her voice suddenly clear.

Hunter listened to her steps echoing in the hallway.

"So, what's really going on?" Amber sounded breathless.

"I was just missing you. And I wanted to see if you can ask mom to excuse you from work one day next week. I want to take you to the Gardens of Luxembourg. The flowers should be blooming now."

"Hunter, this job is important to me. I don't want to take advantage of my relationship with you."

Hunter worried that this conversation was taking a turn in the wrong direction.

"Baby, you don't understand. I need to see more of you." His voice was low and throaty.

"The next few weekends I'm going to have to work at the gallery. But I want to see you for a whole day. Just you and me. I've always loved Paris in Spring and I feel like I'm missing out. Please do this for me, Gorgeous."

"Oh, Hunter," Amber said softly. "Of course I want to be with you as well. I suppose your mother will understand. She did say that it was a shame that work has been taking up so much of your time. I know that it's temporary. But it's awful for me too."

"Thanks, Baby. This will give me something to look forward to while I'm working."

"Me, too, Hunter," Amber said, her voice soft and sensual. "I am glad you called. I think about you all the time as well."

As Hunter hung up, he felt like he had when he had first started dating Amber. There was that little thrill of excitement in knowing that she had agreed to go out with him.

Grinning, he shook his head and headed back to work. Love certainly did strange things to you.

Chapter 33

Finding Amber Holloway's former address proved insanely easy with a few clicks on the internet. Still, Kayla worried she might not find anything in Amber's past that would ruin the girl's relationship with Hunter.

She followed a narrow, mostly empty road out into a remote area where a rundown trailer sat on a neglected lawn full of weeds and rusting car parts. A dented sedan sat off to one side.

Kayla almost didn't get out of the car. This was crazy. Nobody even knew where she was. What if there was a lunatic inside with a gun? She shivered. Anything could happen out here and nobody would ever know.

She could take her chances or drive away without any hope at all for revenge.

Taking a deep breath, Kayla opened the car door and marched up the rickety steps of the neglected porch. With clammy hands and her heart pumping so hard her head ached, she knocked on the door.

Kayla physically recoiled when she saw the occupant.

"I'm not buying whatever it is you're selling."

The woman took a long drag on her cigarette and blew smoke in Kayla's face.

"I'm not here to sell you anything," Kayla managed to say while fighting off a coughing fit.

"I'm here about your daughter Amber."

At the name, the woman scowled. She tugged at the skimpy halter top that barely contained her sagging breasts. She scratched her bare belly that flopped over her short shorts as she stared hard at Kayla.

"The little shit left me here and ran off to college. Hasn't called or visited in months. She's the last person I want to talk about."

The cigarette bobbed in the corner of her mouth as she spoke.

Kayla felt a smile turning up the corners of her mouth even as her eyes watered from the cloud of cigarette smoke in her face.

"Mrs. Holloway, I have some fabulous news for you. I can be your fairy godmother and get you lots of money. But you and I'll have to work together."

Chapter 34

It was mid-morning before Amber and Hunter finally left the hotel suite. Pierre, as usual, was already waiting in the car.

"You have the list?" Hunter asked Pierre as he followed Amber into the car.

"Yes. Just send me a text when you're ready." Pierre gave Amber a small wink.

"What list?" Amber stared from Hunter to Pierre.

"You'll find out soon enough." Hunter smiled and stared out the window.

Amber settled into her seat as Pierre got back into the driver's seat. She wore a new dress. The flowing fabric was printed with blossoms of large pink flowers. A pale pink cardigan sweater kept off the morning chill.

Hunter wore dark jeans, a white button-down shirt, and a gray pullover sweater. No matter what he wore, Amber found him handsome.

Seeing her staring at him, he grinned.

"Do I meet your approval?"

"Very much." Amber slid her hand in his.

As she stared out at the passing scenery, Amber thought she was beginning to see what life for working couples must be like. Between her job, Hunter's internship at the gallery, and the odd hours he spent helping his father out at the company, she felt as though they hardly saw each other lately.

And yet, Amber had to admit that her version of life was quite pampered compared to most couples. After all, she didn't have to work if she didn't want to. A driver escorted her to any location she desired, even on short notice. She knew that ordinary couples didn't have the luxury of eating out in nice restaurants for dinner and ordering in nutritious lunches without much thought for the cost.

For not the first time, Amber marveled at how easily she now took those things for granted. A part of her felt guilty for enjoying such pleasures. Working as a cashier at the grocery store seemed like another life. But yet it was less than a year when she had been working on her feet for long hours and agonizing over every penny she spent.

What if she woke up one day and found that it had all been a dream?

She pinched herself and felt the sharp pain in her thigh. Well, it certainly felt real enough for the moment. She might as well enjoy the experience while she could. She leaned against Hunter and he put an arm around her shoulder.

He seemed lost in his thoughts. But then again, she didn't feel particularly chatty herself at the moment. She rested her cheek against his chest. His cologne was light and mingled with his own earthy smell and the soft scent of soap. With a pang, she realized that he rarely smelled like paint or turpentine anymore.

She knew that Hunter was getting assigned increasingly important responsibilities at the gallery, but she had to wonder if he missed his painting.

Hunter tapped her shoulder and motioned out the window. He pointed out the Luxembourg Palace in the distance.

"The French Senate actually owns the garden," Hunter was saying, "and they meet in the Palace. We'll probably see a lot of police around."

Pierre pulled up at the gate and hurried to open the back door. Hunter extended his hand and helped Amber from the car. When she saw how extensive the grounds were, she was glad that she had worn sensible, comfortable flats.

"It's so lovely," Amber said after they had leisurely walked around, stopping frequently to admire statues and the blooming flowers.

"The next time we come, I'm going to bring a sketch pad."

"Good idea," Hunter said, lightly taking her hand again.

"Let's head this way. I want to show you the most famous fountain here."

Suddenly, though, he stopped. Letting go of her hand, Hunter pulled his phone out of his back pocket.

"Do me a favor and stand by that statue over there. I want to get a picture of you."

As he fiddled with the phone, Amber stepped over to one of the numerous statues. She shifted her hips to make her figure look better before propping one hand on the cool stone.

The sun was so bright, though, that she couldn't keep her eyes open. She fished in her bag for her sunglasses.

"Sorry, but I don't want to be squinting in the picture," she called out.

"Doesn't matter, baby. You are still just as beautiful."

Once Hunter had gotten his photo, he took Amber's hand again and they continued walking.

"The fountain is called the Medici Fountain," he explained. "Very famous. If I remember correctly, the widow of King

Henry IV of France had it built. I know it was renovated a couple hundred years after that and at some point it was moved from its original location."

A little while later, Amber and Hunter passed yet again in front of the Palace. But this time they were taking the main path in front, keeping the Palace on their left as they continued walking. It was now approaching noon. Many more visitors milled about in spite of it being the middle of the week.

"Many of these people live in the surrounding neighborhood," Hunter said. "You can usually spot the tourists. They tend to walk around with their cameras the whole time. In the summer, the crowds get much bigger."

"It must be wonderful to simply walk out your door and come here," Amber said. "Except for Central Park, I can't even imagine that in most places in the States."

While most people simply walked, Amber noticed several joggers and even a few people cycling past. Several minutes later, they stepped off the path where a large number of tourists had collected to take photographs of the fountain.

They approached from the side and Amber could see it was a sizable structure. There was a rectangular shaped pool. The still, black water reflected trees, a few clouds, and surrounding structures. Raised barriers running the length of the pool were topped with decorative urns. But most compelling was the raised structure at the foot of the pool.

Here was built what looked like the front facade and four decorative columns of a Greek building. In the middle of the porch area was an elevated boulder from which a large Greek figure crouched. He stared menacingly at two lovers below him. The male figure was seated and holding his lover in his arms as she reclined against him.

Like most Greek statues, the lovers were mostly naked. But it was the intimacy of their pose that Amber found most fascinating. The lovers looked as if they had been caught in the moment and simply frozen in time.

"Who are they supposed to be?" Amber maneuvered as close to the figures as she could.

"The guy is Acis. Galatea, the sea nymph, is his lover. But the big dude on top of the boulder is a cyclops named Polyphemus. He was jealous and wanted Galatea for himself. So he killed Acis with a boulder. The story says that Galatea turned his blood into the Acis River in Sicily."

"That's rather morbid," Amber said with a grimace.

Hunter stuck his hands in his pockets.

"I remember being afraid of Polyphemus when I was little. But I thought Galatea was quite beautiful. I pretended that Polyphemus fell off the rock and knocked himself out. And that Acis escaped with Galatea."

Amber grinned. "That's definitely a more child-friendly ending. I didn't realize you were a romantic at such an early age."

"Baby, I've been working on my technique for years and years. That's why I'm so good."

Amber laughed.

"And humble as well."

She took out her cell phone and snapped a few photographs.

"They look so lifelike," she marveled. "The artistry is amazing. The pose is so natural and the details are so specific."

Hunter's phone beeped with a message and Amber saw him glance at the screen for a moment before stuffing it back into his pocket.

"I'm afraid we need to go and meet Pierre."

Amber tried not to show her disappointment. Had the gallery decided that they needed Hunter to work that afternoon?

"Perhaps next time we can stay a bit longer. I wouldn't mind bringing a book and sitting out in the sun."

"Sounds like a good plan," Hunter said. "But before we go, I have one more stop I'd like to show you."

Amber took his hand. But her pleasure was quickly waning. She had looked forward to having an entire day with Hunter. She had to plaster a fake smile on her face as Hunter pointed out more statues along the path.

Too soon, they turned a corner and were back on the main path. A little further down was a wide expanse of green lawn where large groups had already congregated to sit, eat, and soak up the sun.

Hunter took her hand and they wove through the settled crowd until Pierre waved them over.

"Oh! What a nice surprise!" Amber's spirits lifted.

Pierre had spread out a large checkered blanket and arranged a bottle of wine, and plates of cheese, meats, breads, and sweets. There was even a single red rose on one of the plates.

"Well done, Pierre." Hunter shook the man's hand.

"Why don't you go and take a long lunch. I'll give you a call when we are done."

Amber almost missed seeing him slip a large bill into Pierre's hand. She was glad to know that the driver's extra efforts were being rewarded appropriately.

After Pierre disappeared, Amber sat down to enjoy her picnic.

"You really surprised me," she said after they had devoured half the food.

"When you started texting, I thought you had to go back to work."

Hunter sank back on his elbows and closed his eyes.

"Wild horses couldn't drag me back to work."

Amber smiled as she packed up the last of the food and set it aside so that they would have room to stretch out together on the blanket. She slipped off her shoes and wiggled her toes.

As she snuggled against Hunter and sipped her wine, she thought about how life couldn't get much more perfect than this.

Chapter 35

Mrs. Holloway stepped back and held the door open, motioning for Kayla to follow her in.

"The maid hasn't shown up in a while."

She waved her bare arms at the messy living room.

Kayla cringed and wished she could walk right back out the door. Worse than the heavily soiled carpet, overflowing ashtrays, or beer cans littering the tables was the stench of stale smoke, body odor, and soured milk.

"The kitchen is cleaner."

Mrs. Holloway stepped over soiled laundry and continued through the cramped space.

The smell of spoiled milk was worse in the kitchen. But the table was miraculously clean. The sink, however, overflowed with dirty dishes.

"Would you like a beer?"

Mrs. Holloway opened the fridge and pulled out a can for herself.

"No, but thank you."

Kayla tried to ignore the stench and focus on her task.

Think of the final prize. Ruining Amber.

"Have a seat." Mrs. Holloway plopped into a chair and lit another cigarette.

The harsh fluorescent lights illuminated her haggard face. Years of over tanning gave her skin a leathery appearance. Her lips had that wrinkled look many long-term smokers sported.

Heavy bags hung from below her bloodshot eyes. Gray roots showed from oily hair that hung limply around her face.

Still, Kayla could see that the woman had once been attractive. With a decent haircut, proper skin care, makeup, and appropriate clothing, she might even be presentable. That would be important.

"So I'm guessing that you don't know that your daughter is dating a very wealthy man right now," she said, getting directly to the point.

"Wealthy?"

Kayla smiled as the woman's entire body straightened a notch.

"That's right. It's a shame that a mother gets abandoned while her only daughter runs around Paris getting pampered like a princess."

"She's always been ungrateful," Mrs. Holloway said bitterly. "Always thinking about her needs. She knows that I'm disabled and can't work."

Kayla suspected that alcohol was Mrs. Holloway's major disability. But she kept that thought to herself. Frankly, she didn't care what happened to the woman in the long run. But a disgruntled mother could be made to look quite sympathetic to the media. And a sympathetic media could embarrass the Webbs. It would be a simple step to plant the seed of belief that Amber had flung herself at Hunter for his money.

But no media outlet was going to care about this hag sitting in front of her. Mrs. Holloway required molding.

"If you want this to work, you'll have to do everything I ask." Kayla's voice hardened.

"But I promise you'll get what you deserve in the end."

Mrs. Holloway's eyes glittered. "Tell me more."

Chapter 36

Uncharacteristically, Hunter's fingers trembled as he signed the hotel register.

"Are you okay, Mr. Webb?" The clerk looked alarmed.

"Fine. Too much coffee this morning." Hunter forced a smile.

He was going to have to get his emotions in check or Amber was going to figure out something was awry. Fortunately, she was off to the side admiring the colorful fish in the hotel's elaborate aquarium.

"All set," he said a few minutes later, wiping sweat from his brow.

"I see the humidity is getting to you, too."

Amber punched the button on the elevator.

"Yeah, definitely not used to that," Hunter agreed, relieved that she attributed his discomfort to the weather.

He shielded his hands at the door so that Amber could not see him fumble with the room key.

"Very pretty!" Amber remarked, moving past him to inspect the room.

The room wasn't fancy compared to the expensive hotel suite in Paris, but Hunter had purposely not booked the most luxurious hotel.

Amber would never have believed that a business trip warranted such luxury. And right now she completely believed that business was the only reason that they were here in Houston, Texas.

Choosing this location had taken him ages. First he had to find a city that his father legitimately had business in. Just in case Amber asked around at work. The second consideration had been weather. He didn't want to freeze. Houston was one of the few cities that met both criteria.

Still, as far as conference hotels went, this one was quite nice. It offered both an indoor and outdoor pool for its guests as well as a spa. Hunter had already booked both of them a massage for later that afternoon. He was hoping that the relaxation would quell his nerves.

For the umpteenth time, he waited until Amber was looking away and patted his jacket pocket to reassure himself. Yes, the small box was still there.

"Why don't you change into some shorts," Amber said, pulling out water bottles from the refrigerator and handing him one.

"Good idea," Hunter said. "Maybe I'll just hop in the shower first and wash off some of this sweat."

"Good idea." Amber rolled her suitcase past him to the second bedroom.

"Maybe we can hang out by the pool a little before dinner."

"Very tempting," Hunter said, following her and bending to give her a kiss. "But I told the company representative that I'd meet him as soon as we arrived."

Amber pouted. "But I thought your conference didn't start until tomorrow."

"Trust me. I'd much rather be having fun with you than talking about boring company matters."

"Do you want me to tag along?"

Hunter's stomach heaved as he was overcome with a moment of panic. What if Amber sneaked downstairs and discovered his secret?

"What? And have some other guy staring at my beautiful girl while I'm stuck talking business."

He smiled and kissed her once more.

"Besides, I would be staring at you the whole time."

Fortunately, Amber laughed.

"Okay, just don't stay gone too long. We still have our massages this afternoon, right?"

Relieved, Hunter swiftly started to unpack the suitcases.

"Don't worry. I'll be back in plenty of time for that."

Amber pushed his hands away when he started to remove her things.

"I can do that. Go and get ready for your meeting. The sooner you meet up with your client, the sooner we can have some alone time."

Grabbing clean clothes, Hunter headed for the shower. Any more alone time with Amber was going to be difficult. Every time he saw her face, he pictured himself on his knees with the ring. If she didn't agree to marry him, he wasn't sure how he was going to survive.

Once he was showered and changed, he nearly bolted from the room.

Chapter 37

Kayla didn't have high hopes when she returned to visit Mrs. Holloway. She had given the woman a large list of things to do. Frankly, she wondered if the woman was sober and responsible enough to carry out half of what she had asked of her.

She had been quite busy herself, mostly in dealing with the bank executives. Fortunately, her lawyers in Paris had managed to persuade the courts that Kayla needed financial support. Some of her parent's assets had been unfrozen and placed in her own accounts. Still, the amount of money released would cover only her basic living expenses for the next two years. Beyond that, she would have to live well beneath what she was accustomed to.

Worse, though, the courts had assigned an accountant to manage her expenses. Anything beyond what was considered a reasonable living expense had to be justified. Apparently, weekly manicures, pedicures, and outings with her girlfriends did not count as a living expense. Instead, a monthly entertainment and personal expense allotment of a thousand dollars was given to her.

"You're very fortunate," the accountant gushed. "That's very generous."

"Obviously, you shop at bargain stores, get your hair styled at cheap salons, and only eat at fast food restaurants," Kayla snapped.

Now she had to spend some of that precious money on rehabilitating Amber's mother. Just one more reason for Kayla to hate the girl who had ruined her life.

Sighing, she got out of her car and approached the door. This time, though, she didn't even have a chance to knock.

"Come in!" Mrs. Holloway said cheerfully. "You'll see what a difference I've made in such a short amount of time."

Kayla was glad to see that the woman wasn't waving around one of her disgusting cigarettes. But she groaned inwardly as she noticed that the woman was still wearing inappropriate clothing.

"I see you admiring my new clothes. I just got these new things last week."

Kayla managed to bite back a sarcastic reply.

She viewed Mrs. Holloway's clothing with a critical eye. The jeans were an improvement over the short shorts. But they were so tight that they created a pathetic muffin top that bulged beneath her mid-drift blouse. The woman still wasn't wearing a supportive bra and her breasts sagged.

"That's a good step in the right direction," Kayla said carefully. "But we might have to tweak the shirt a bit for interviews. Maybe even consider a conservative dress."

Mrs. Holloway pursed her lips.

"You didn't say I was going to have to lay out a whole bunch of cash for new clothes. I can only do so much with my limited income."

She looked Kayla up and down. "You seem to have plenty of cash for your wardrobe."

Kayla sighed.

"I suppose I can give you a small clothing allowance. Or better yet, we'll go shopping together and find a few good outfits. Especially something for when the reporters come by."

Mrs. Holloway put her hands on her hips.

"I still don't see how you're going to get the newspapers interested."

"Just leave that to me. For now, why don't we see what still needs to be done around the house."

Although the trailer still smelled rank with stale smoke, the ashtrays had at least been emptied. The empty beer cans had disappeared and it looked as though the furniture had even been dusted.

"Nice job cleaning up. But remember to put away anything smoking related when reporters come by. You don't want them talking about you wasting money on cigarettes when we are trying to make you seem like you can barely afford groceries."

She thought that Mrs. Holloway would be offended. Instead, the woman simply nodded her head sagely.

"I'd better hide the empty beer cans. Got hundreds out back."

"Good idea." Kayla moved into the kitchen.

The sink was grubby. But at least it wasn't piled high with dishes.

"Them there are hard water deposits," said Mrs. Holloway defensively as she saw Kayla inspecting the area.

"We can pick up some special cleaners to take care of that. Shiny sinks impress people."

Kayla peered down the hall. "What about the bathroom?"

"What do I need to show people my bathroom for?"

Kayla fought to keep her temper.

"You don't have to show them every room. But eventually somebody from out of town is going to have to relieve themselves. It's a long way from the airport and not a lot of places to stop and pee on the way."

"Oh," said Mrs. Holloway, mollified. "Well, it ain't ready today. Took me forever to get this much done. I ain't a young thing like you."

She studied Kayla with a glitter in her eyes.

"Maybe you could come over and clean with me one afternoon."

Kayla nearly laughed out loud. She stopped herself just in time.

"Sorry, but I'm allergic to cleaners," she said, lying smoothly.

After all, she didn't even clean her own bathroom. She sure as hell wasn't cleaning up after Amber's mother.

Mrs. Holloway didn't look like she believed her. But she didn't push the issue.

"So we're close to being ready?"

Kayla studied the woman. Mrs. Holloway had managed to wash her hair. But the roots and poor cut looked terrible.

"Can you color your own hair?"

"What makes you think I need to?" Mrs. Holloway asked, defensive once again.

"You just have a couple of roots showing," Kayla said, trying not to roll her eyes.

Mrs. Holloway's eyes glittered again. She smiled slyly.

"I used to be able to color it myself when I was younger. But now my hands get too stiff."

Kayla realized with a sinking feeling that Mrs. Holloway was going to get all she could out of this arrangement.

"Fine. I'll pay for a cut and color rinse in a couple of weeks. But we concentrate on making this place look its best first."

"Looks fine to me," Mrs. Holloway said with a simple shrug. "Unless you want to hire a cleaner to come in."

Kayla had enough. Imitating a look she had endured from her own mother a million times, she lifted her chin and spoke sharply.

"Look. I've got limited funds myself. You need to ask yourself how badly you want to get the public sympathetic to your plight. Because I can walk away at any time and cut my losses."

She must have gotten the look right because Mrs. Holloway backed down.

"Okay, okay. No need to get an attitude. You get me some of those special cleaners and I'll finish up the kitchen."

Kayla nodded.

"I'll bring some by tomorrow. I'll also rent a steam cleaner for the carpets."

She looked around the home.

"Just remember what our end goal is here. And also all the work I'm doing on my end."

Mrs. Holloway laughed suddenly.

"What?" Kayla asked.

"Nothing, really," Mrs. Holloway said, still chuckling. "I was just thinking that you must hate my daughter a lot to go through all this trouble. I only hope it works out for you."

Chapter 38

Amber unpacked the rest of the luggage, smiling as she hung everything neatly in the closet. Hunter's habits were starting to rub off on her.

She hoped that this trip would help them reconnect as a couple. Hunter was always so open. But lately he had retreated inside himself. If they had not had such a great day at the Luxembourg Gardens a few weeks earlier, she would have really begun to question their relationship. Instead, the entire day had been absolutely perfect.

Amber shook her head, trying to dispel the feeling that something was wrong. Surely Hunter was just overwhelmed with work. Maybe it was also the stress of not being able to paint. She would have to suggest that he make time to get back into his art, even if it meant cutting into some of their outings on the weekend.

After all, she still had her stained glass classes. She didn't know the last time Hunter had even made a sketch. And she knew how miserable she had been when not pursuing her art.

Her conscience chimed in, like usual.

Stop creating problems! Enjoy this little trip. Remember how heartbroken Hunter was when you broke up with him. He couldn't have possibly changed that much so soon.

Amber put away the last of her folded items. She would wow Hunter with her organizational skills. The shock alone should snap him out of his weird mood.

Chapter 39

Kayla reluctantly plucked down money at a cheap salon for a haircut, coloring, and eyebrow waxing. Even though the price was only a fraction of what she would have paid at her own expensive salon, it burned Kayla that she was paying to make her worst enemy's mother look nice. Afterward, however, she had to admit that the woman looked at least a hundred times better than she had when they entered the establishment.

"I can't believe that's me." Mrs. Holloway gaped at herself in the mirror.

"I'll definitely pick up a better class of men."

Kayla hurriedly paid the bill and ushered Mrs. Holloway out of the building.

"You can't say stuff like that in public," she scolded as they got back in her car.

Mrs. Holloway pulled out a compact and admired herself.

"Darling, I can't stay hidden and quiet now that I look this good."

Kayla slammed her car door shut and groaned.

"Look, you have to behave yourself or this isn't going to work!"

Mrs. Holloway continued to preen in the mirror.

"This color does so much more for my complexion," she marveled.

Kayla started the car.

"I guess I'll just take you back to your place, drop you off, and forget the whole thing."

She adopted her mother's most chilling voice. Low but threatening.

Mrs. Holloway snapped the compact shut and tossed it in her purse.

"No need to get your knickers wadded up. Can't blame a girl for getting excited about a new hairdo."

Kayla didn't say anything and pulled out into traffic.

"We're still going shopping for clothes, right?" Mrs. Holloway sounded contrite.

Kayla kept silent.

"Fine. I'll be good. I won't even date in public until your little plan is finished."

"No dating. Period," Kayla said firmly. "I get one whiff of you even flirting in public and this whole deal is off. You can sit in your dumpy little trailer for the rest of your life while your daughter lives a life of luxury."

Mrs. Holloway waved her hand dismissively.

"You've made your point. I agree to your terms. Now let's go get me something decent to wear for those reporters that you are so convinced are going to turn up."

Kayla turned into the nearest discount store parking lot.

"Two dresses. And one pair of nice sandals. That's all you should need."

Once in the store, Kayla found Mrs. Holloway to be even more exasperating.

"No," she said sharply for the fourth time. "No spaghetti straps. No low cut dresses. Nothing that doesn't at least drop down to your knees."

"But I'm going to look like an old lady," Mrs. Holloway complained. "No man is going to look twice at me if I look like a grandmother."

Kayla gritted her teeth and rubbed her aching head.

"The idea is to make you look helpless. I want you looking like an innocent church woman."

"You want me to start going to church then?"

The idea had merit for a few moments. Kayla started to agree and then pictured Mrs. Holloway flirting with a pastor.

"No. Let's just keep to the basics. We don't want to make this more complicated than it already is."

Finally, Mrs. Holloway agreed to two simple dresses. Although one was loud, it at least covered up her sagging breasts.

"Now, go in there and try on these bras," Kayla said, thrusting a couple at the woman.

"I don't like bras," Mrs. Holloway confessed. "They don't feel natural."

"Well, natural boobs flopping out of control are going to hurt our cause," Kayla said evenly. "And if I feel our cause is threatened..."

She didn't need to finish. Mrs. Holloway grabbed the bras and headed for the changing room.

"Well, I'll be," she announced in a gravelly voice. "These make my girls look years younger."

Kayla smacked her forehead. It would be a miracle if she pulled this off. But when Mrs. Holloway walked out a few minutes later, she had to agree that the woman looked nice.

The dress was modest enough even with Mrs. Holloway's ample bosom. If she could train the woman to say the right things in an interview, they might be successful after all. In fact, Kayla decided to start the prep work that very afternoon.

Chapter 40

After secretly leaving the hotel, Hunter took a cab to the bay side restaurant where he had made reservations. He checked in with the restaurant staff and made final arrangements to have flowers and champagne delivered to the table if Amber said yes. Finally, when he had been assured that all would go perfectly, Hunter returned to the hotel.

But he didn't go back to the room right away. Instead, he spent time just staring out at the pool. He thought back to the very first time he had seen Amber fainting at school. Even then, she had felt right in his arms. She had always been beautiful to him. But he had since learned just how smart and tough and funny she was.

He loved how Amber never put on any airs or acted like she was better than anyone else. She was simply herself. So why was he so rattled right now? This was the right decision. The only thing left to do now was to actually drop to one knee and propose.

He had originally tried to think of some clever way to produce the ring. But he could barely manage the traditional proposal. He would just play it safe. Go for the traditional knee drop.

What if she rejected him?

Then you ask her again in a few months. And you keep asking until she agrees.

Hunter's watch beeped and he jumped. But it was only the reminder for their massages. He hurried to the elevator, not wanting to make Amber sore. He knew he was acting weird. Showing up late wasn't going to make her feel any better. And he wanted her in a good mood for the evening.

"Sorry I'm getting back so late."

Amber used her finger as a place marker and glanced up from her book.

"Not a problem," she said agreeably.

She flexed her feet, showing off newly painted toenails.

"I've been wanting to start this novel for a while. I think I'll take it to the pool tomorrow while you're at your meeting."

"Sounds good," Hunter said, leaning over to give her a peck on the cheek.

A half hour later, he tried to relax.

"You've got some serious stress knots," said the massage therapist working on his back. "Is it okay if I apply a little more pressure?"

"Go ahead," Hunter said, trying to will his mind into submission.

The discomfort gave his mind a welcome distraction.

"Stay and relax a bit if you like. The shower and dressing rooms are just down the hall on your left."

"Thanks."

After the therapist left the room, Hunter sat up immediately and put on the robe and slippers left for him. Normally, he felt relaxed and warm after a massage. But today he felt charged. He found himself counting down the minutes until they would leave for the restaurant.

After showering and dressing, Hunter made his way back to the waiting room. He checked his phone for texts and e-mail but couldn't concentrate. He tried to read a magazine. But halfway through, he realized he had no idea what the article was about. Finally, he stood and paced.

"Everything okay?" an elderly gentleman asked with concern.

Hunter tried to smile.

"Sorry. I'm on edge because I'm going to propose to my girlfriend this evening."

The man smiled.

"If it makes you feel any better, your reaction is quite normal. Sort of a rite of passage. Years later, you'll laugh about it with your wife."

"At the moment I just feel sick and antsy," Hunter confessed.

"I'll send good thoughts your way." The man tilted his head toward the door.

"Is that your young lady?"

Hunter gave the man an appreciative nod and then hurried to leave with Amber. He was anxious to get back to the room. He was aware of how little time they had before the car service picked them up.

Fortunately, Amber had already dried and styled her hair in the spa dressing room. It hung around her shoulders in soft waves. She looked incredibly beautiful even in shorts and a tee shirt. He couldn't wait to see her in the new black dress he had spotted in her garment bag.

"How was your massage, Gorgeous?"

"Wonderful. I nodded off toward the end."

"Me too," Hunter lied.

He had an insane desire to jog back to the room. Every nerve in his body buzzed as if he was plugged into an electrical outlet.

Instead, he simply took Amber's hand and forced himself to remain calm as they walked at what seemed like a snail's pace back to the room.

Chapter 41

Sitting in her own home in front of a pile of containers of her favorite Thai food takeout, Kayla smiled as she put down her cell phone.

The local paper was thrilled to have a scoop about the Webb family. True, the paper was obscure. But Kayla was certain that other papers might pick up the story. Unless the assigned reporter screwed things up. But Kayla was going to make sure that it was the kind of story that appealed to the masses.

She had spent the afternoon coaxing Mrs. Holloway on what to say. She had even given the woman a cheat sheet to study over the next few days. Just to be on the safe side, Kayla had arranged for the reporter to come the following week. As much as she wanted to ruin Hunter and Amber's lives as quickly as possible, Kayla didn't want to make the mistake of presenting Mrs. Holloway before she had been properly groomed.

If all went well, the papers would gain traction. Once they did, Kayla was prepared to present the Webbs with an offer to make the bad press disappear. For a hefty price.

As she helped herself to seconds, Kayla went over the major points she wanted the paper to cover.

Amber Holloway runs away from her devoted, destitute mother to cavort with her playboy boyfriend Hunter Webb in Paris. The daughter lives a life of riches while the mother relies on welfare. Amber Holloway is obviously a gold digger since she started going after the wealthy Hunter Webb on the very first day of college, pretending to be injured to get his attention. She has had no contact with her mother and has not once inquired about her health or welfare.

For the first time in months, Kayla allowed herself a very real laugh. She couldn't wait to see how this played out in the media.

Chapter 42

Amber felt relaxed and at ease after her wonderful massage that afternoon. Now she was wearing a cute new black dress she had chosen in Paris. The lines were simple, but the cut fit her perfectly. To dress it up she wore, as always, her emerald bracelet from Hunter, simple silver earrings, and black heels. She also carried a small silver purse, a recent gift from Hunter's mom.

Their table looked directly out onto the bay. The sun was in the midst of setting and tinges of pink and orange streaked the horizon.

Amber studied Hunter as he sipped his wine. Even though the restaurant was cool, he had beads of sweat across his forehead. Was he coming down with a cold from the plane?

But of course he looked as handsome as ever. His hair was slightly tousled in front where he had been fidgeting with it earlier. And his green eyes sparkled in the dim light of the candle. He wore a charcoal gray suit with a crisp white shirt open at the throat.

Amber had a sudden desire to lean over and kiss that little hollow on his neck. In fact, she had been thinking about kissing him all day. Now, he sat there watching her silently, almost broodingly.

"Excuse me a second." Hunter rose quickly and left in the direction of the restrooms.

Amber watched him with more concern. This was the third time he had gotten up since they were seated. She would suggest that they go back to the room and save dinner for another night.

But when he returned a few minutes later, Hunter looked perfectly fine. Extremely focused, she thought, as he sat down and took a large gulp of wine.

"Are you okay?"

"I've been meaning to ask you something."

Hunter slid off his chair and knelt on the floor. He reached into his jacket pocket, pulled out a box and opened it.

"I've been in love with you since the first time I ever laid eyes on you. Amber Holloway, will you marry me?"

Amber felt her mouth drop. She had never in a million years expected this to happen this night. Especially when she thought that Hunter was growing distant. But he was really there in front of her, his eyes eager and anxious at the same time.

She found her voice as her hands extended in the direction of the ring.

"Yes," she said with a gasp. "I mean. I love you too. Of course I'll marry you!"

As Hunter slid the ring on her finger and Amber bent to kiss him, the entire restaurant began to clap.

Hunter slipped back into his chair, his smile wide.

"Congratulations!" the waiter said, appearing almost immediately with a vase of red roses.

The manager was only a step behind with a bottle of champagne.

"Compliments of the house. We wish you the best."

"Thank you," Amber murmured, overcome.

She felt like she was in a dream. But it was important to try to capture and remember every moment of this night. She stared down at the ring on her finger, realizing for the first time that it was an emerald surrounded by a tiny cluster of diamonds.

She was engaged!

Chapter 43

In spite of the carpet cleaning, Mrs. Holloway's trailer still smelled strongly of stale smoke.

"I don't see any other way around it," Kayla said as she inspected the yellowed walls.

"You're going to have to wash these down with some detergent."

"What? All of them?" Mrs. Holloway's eyebrows shot up in disbelief. "I couldn't do all that work before tomorrow even if I wanted to. Why don't I just spray some more air freshener?"

Kayla surveyed the room, her head starting to throb. She couldn't let that reporter in here with this stench. She wished she had thought to have Mrs. Holloway meet the woman somewhere else. But then, the trailer was part of the story she needed to have people see.

She would not let everything fall apart now. Not after all the time and money spent preparing for Amber's mother to tell her sad little sob story. No, she was going to have to resort to extreme measures. Too bad she didn't have extra money. But she had already had to let her own housekeeper go the week before.

"I can't believe I'm saying this, but I'll help you," Kayla said resignedly. "We'll have to clean the curtains and furniture as well."

Mrs. Holloway laughed and it sounded like a small dog barking.

"You? Have you ever cleaned anything in your life? You and your fancy car and clothes and attitude?"

Kayla gave the woman a vicious look.

"Sometimes we all have to do things we don't like."

"Good for you, darling. You have more gumption than I thought you did."

Mrs. Holloway turned and headed for the kitchen.

"I have a couple of cleaning buckets and sponges in here. You might want to put on a pair of gloves over those manicured hands."

Kayla didn't speak. While Mrs. Holloway made preparations to clean the walls, she took down the grimy curtains hanging in the window. They looked like cheap ones that could probably be machine washed.

"Go ahead and put these in while we do the walls. And better get the ones in the kitchen as well. Add a cup of vinegar to the wash. I read on the internet it would help take out odors."

An hour later, sweat ran down Kayla's face as she washed down the walls beside Mrs. Holloway. The woman had actually been correct about her never having done any physical labor. Her back hurt and she was sure at least one nail was broken.

Still, she got grim satisfaction thinking about how all of this work was going to bring suffering to both Hunter and Amber. By the end of the day, she was exhausted and her clothes were filthy from cleaning. But the walls were much brighter and the smell of smoke had diminished, especially after they had sprinkled large amounts of baking soda all over the sofa and chair cushions.

"Wait until tomorrow morning to vacuum them off," Kayla said. "And I don't want you to smoke even one single cigarette in this place. Take your filthy habit outside."

"I'm not an idiot," grumbled Mrs. Holloway.

Kayla suspected the woman's ill mood was due to not smoking or drinking all day. She wondered how long it had been since the woman had remained sober this long.

"Just keep looking at the reward at the end of the day," Kayla said more gently, not wanting the woman to crack.

She couldn't risk Mrs. Holloway going nuts and getting drunk right before the interview.

"Remember that I'm making sacrifices as well."

Mrs. Holloway snorted and moved to the back of the trailer.

"Curtains are done," she reported, returning with an armful of material.

Once the curtains were back up, Kayla and Mrs. Holloway stood back and surveyed the room.

"Windows look kind of dirty," Mrs. Holloway said, not looking Kayla in the eyes.

Kayla sighed.

"Do you have any window cleaner?"

While Kayla cleaned the inside of the windows, she made Mrs. Holloway tackle the outside. But when they were done, she was glad they had taken the extra effort.

However, now that the sun could shine through, the sofa and chairs looked even grimier than before.

"I don't suppose you have any furniture covers," Kayla said, already knowing the answer.

Mrs. Holloway just stared at her.

Kayla sighed again. Any more purchases and she would have to forgo takeout for the rest of the month. She would have to actually cook her own food. Was getting back at Hunter and Amber worth this much effort?

She closed her eyes and made herself picture the way that Hunter gazed adoringly at Amber. She made herself remember her mother's look of disgust when she found out that Hunter had no interest in her daughter.

Opening her eyes, she clenched her fists and strengthened her resolve.

"Get in the car. We'll have to go shopping. Remind me to get some plug in air fresheners as well."

Chapter 44

Hunter couldn't keep the silly grin off his face as he stared at Amber across the table. She was now his fiancée.

"Is the ring okay?"

"It's stunning. The emerald is so unique. It will always have special meaning to me. And I'm glad you went with silver."

"Mom and Dad's wedding bands are silver. I guess I was being a little sentimental."

He squeezed her hand to make sure he was still awake. He still couldn't get over how he was now an engaged man.

Amber smiled suddenly.

"I was really worried about you before. You were acting so weird. When you kept going to the restroom, I thought that you were coming down with the flu."

Hunter laughed.

"I was so nervous. I'm sorry for being so distant. Every time I looked at you, I thought I was going to blurt out the whole thing and ruin the surprise. And tonight I had myself so worked up I couldn't stop sweating."

"But you knew I would say yes!"

"I hoped so. But we've never really discussed it. I was afraid you might think that it was too soon after our little separation."

Amber looked down and twisted the ring on her finger.

"That was a rough time. But it made me realize just how much I love and need you."

Hunter leaned forward and took Amber's hand in his.

"I know that all couples have challenges. But I promise that I'll always be there for you."

Amber's eyes grew moist.

"I know, Hunter. That's one of the things I love about you."

Chapter 45

Kayla stared dubiously at the small container of food she pulled from the microwave. Although she had followed the directions, the meal looked overcooked. The edges of the plastic container held gummy bits of sauce. The chicken, when she tried to cut it, felt rubbery. The taste was only marginally better than the appearance.

But she was hungry and her checking account was shockingly low. How did people live on so little money? For the first time in her life, Kayla was scared. Even if he avoided jail time, her father was out of a job. Debt and legal fees were going to wipe out most of her parents' savings. There was even discussion of prosecution for tax evasion. Things looked bad.

And what about her? She wasn't even a college graduate yet. She had always assumed that she would be taken care of financially until she got married. Now her parents advocated getting a job.

She pushed away her plate, suddenly not hungry anymore. A job? Who would hire her? She was certainly not going to take some minimum wage job. She hadn't been raised to lower herself like that.

To cheer herself up, Kayla read the small article in the local paper once again. She couldn't believe that the editor had buried the story inside. Still, the writer had done a nice job of making Mrs. Holloway appear sympathetic. Too bad it was only a couple of paragraphs. Hopefully, a bigger outlet would pick up on the story. Kayla had already commented on the online article herself, anonymously of course, in the hopes of driving more attention to it.

She still had hope that Amber and Hunter's happiness might be destroyed.

As studied the online article, an advertisement popped up in the lower corner of her screen.

New Agency seeking local Models. Will train. No experience necessary.

Kayla clicked the link.

Chapter 46

Amber stared at the samples of wedding invitations with less excitement than most newly engaged women. The problem wasn't that she couldn't find something nice. Or that she was having trouble deciding. No, the difficulty was her family. Or lack of to be precise. How was she going to explain missing parents to their guests?

"Can we put this one in the pile of possibles?"

Hunter held up an embossed card with elegant silver script. He dropped it when he saw her face.

"Are you crying? What's wrong?"

Amber brushed away the few tears that had escaped.

"I'm just being ridiculous, I suppose. I was just thinking about my mom."

Hunter put his arm around her.

"You know that I would fly her here if you wanted."

"Good grief! No!" Amber exclaimed. "Besides, I can't imagine her wanting to come even if I invited her."

Hunter opened his mouth, paused, and closed it again. Then he just waited.

"I know what you're thinking. Part of you still thinks that there might be a shred of decency in her."

"Well, for something big like this? Maybe it would make her rethink her life?"

Amber shook her head. She held up a hand so she could tick off the opportunities her mother had passed by.

"She never went to a single school play. She skipped all my parent teacher conferences. She wouldn't even sign my report cards. I had to forge her name because the teachers wouldn't believe me. She refused to come to my high school graduation. Or to the awards ceremony when I won a small scholarship."

Hunter stared at her with watery eyes.

"I'm so sorry."

Amber smiled grimly.

"At least she didn't have any pretenses of love or affection for me. I knew where I stood with her."

Hunter moved to embrace her.

"And yet you seem upset," he said gently.

"Not upset that she won't be here," Amber said emphatically. "Just upset at the predicament that it puts me in."

"Which is?" Hunter nuzzled his head against her shoulder.

"I'm afraid that people will ask about her or my father. And I don't want to have to explain that on my wedding day."

Hunter was quiet.

What was he thinking? Was he regretting getting engaged to someone with such a dysfunctional family?

"Would you rather have a private ceremony?"

Hunter shifted so he could look her in the face.

"Just my parents and a few friends? People that already know your situation?"

"But I don't want you to sacrifice," Amber murmured. "Won't your parents be disappointed?"

"Gorgeous, I would marry you outside, in the middle of a snowstorm, dressed in a bunny costume if that was what you wanted."

Amber laughed. "Really? In a snowstorm?"

Hunter bent and kissed her.

"So you like the bunny costume idea?"

"You would make an adorable bunny."

"I'm serious, Amber. All I care about is marrying you. And making you happy. However or wherever that happens is completely secondary to me."

Amber blinked back more tears. "But your mom . . ."

Hunter grinned. "Mom was afraid I might not ever get married. Trust me, she won't be picky."

"So she wouldn't be opposed to the bunny costume?"

"Let's not get carried away."

Hunter kissed her again.

Amber let herself be swept away in just being with the person she loved.

Chapter 47

Kayla was in line at the grocery store when she saw the story splashed as a major headline on a tabloid newspaper. Okay, so it wasn't a reputable paper. But it was news!

Kayla grinned as she grabbed two copies. She was even willing to purchase one for Mrs. Holloway. She still couldn't believe that the woman had remained sober long enough to help pull this whole thing off.

She pulled into Mrs. Holloway's driveway in great spirits.

"Kayla? I wasn't expecting you today."

Mrs. Holloway stared at her through the open door. Her eyes were bloodshot and she wore a flimsy bathrobe that stopped mid thigh.

"Is that a beer?" Kayla deflated.

"Just one lousy beer. Don't go and get all high and mighty on me. I deserve it after all the work I've done on your behalf."

She took a long swig from the can and belched.

"What if another reporter comes by? We talked about this. You can't be seen drinking when you open your door."

Kayla hadn't expected to Mrs. Holloway to keep her act clean indefinitely. But this was ridiculous.

"I came to show you the article that got printed in one of the tabloids. But you obviously don't care."

Kayla stomped back down the steps and yanked open her car door.

"Wait! I do want to see."

Mrs. Holloway stumbled down from the porch wobbled across the lawn.

"It's just been a tough week. This is only my second beer today."

"Yeah, right!" Kayla spit out. "That's why you can barely walk."

"Just let me see the article. I'll be better from here on out."

Kayla shoved the paper out the car window and waited.

"I look good in print," was the first thing Mrs. Holloway said.

She chuckled as she continued reading the story.

"Oh, that's good! They did a fine job."

She turned her attention to Kayla.

"And you reckon the family will pay cash to keep me quiet?"

"If they are smart, they will," Kayla said, catching Mrs. Holloway's excitement. "But remember our deal. I get a fifty percent cut of whatever they offer you."

"Sure. Sure," Mrs. Holloway said, her eyes squinting.

"But I think we need to renegotiate your cut. Seems like it's me in the papers rather than you."

"You wouldn't *be* in the papers without me," Kayla said, seething.

She couldn't believe that this woman was going to try to double cross her.

"And remember that they haven't even contacted you yet. What if a lawyer for the Webbs stops by and finds you drunk? How do you think that's going to go for you? Do you have your own lawyer to read the paperwork they'll ask you to sign?"

Mrs. Holloway eyed Kayla warily. But she looked cold and calculating.

"Don't go getting your panties in a wad. I just got a little carried away. We can keep the original agreement."

"Make sure you remember that the next time I drop by," Kayla said, allowing a little nastiness to creep into her voice.

"I've seen you away from the cameras. Pull something against me and I'll make you regret it."

"Oh, come now. Let's let bygones be bygones. Come have a chat. I haven't even smoked inside."

Kayla shook her head.

"I've got other plans. And next time don't open the door until you know who is there. If you aren't dressed properly or the house is a mess, pretend you're not home. Whoever is there will come back later."

"Got you, darling. You be safe going home now."

As Kayla drove away, she had a sinking feeling that she could no longer trust Mrs. Holloway. She could only hope that the events already set in motion would be enough.

Chapter 48

Hunter knew something was wrong as soon as he stepped into his father's office. He hadn't seen his dad look that serious since discovering that the senior accountant was stealing company secrets.

"What is it?"

Mr. Webb sighed.

"Something that is bound to upset Amber. I didn't even want to mention it, but I'm afraid that she'll see it on her own."

"See what?"

"Stories like this one," Mr. Webb said, grasping a paper from his desk and handing it over.

Hunter had to read the title several times before it sank in. Somebody was trying to ruin Amber's reputation. The story made it seem as though she was a money hungry scavenger who had latched onto the Webb family for their wealth.

Hunter cringed as he imagined how Amber would react if she saw the story in a store or overheard somebody talking about it.

"The story is rubbish. Is there anything that legal can do?"

"For now, we should just ignore the story altogether. Officially, we won't even respond to it. I suggest that you and Amber do exactly the same. This is a disreputable rag. From what I can tell, no respectable paper has picked up on the story."

Hunter fumed. "So there's nothing that we can do?"

Mr. Webb held up a hand. "I said officially we do nothing. Obviously, I'll have security look into how the story got started and who may be trying to hurt the family's reputation."

"Do you think it could be Kayla Ross?"

"Why do you think that? Has she contacted with you?"

Hunter shook his head.

"No, but Kayla's the type who would want revenge. She must have been furious that both her parents were charged."

Mr. Webb tapped his chin thoughtfully.

"I imagine that she might be feeling quite overwhelmed and frightened as well. I don't think that her parents' finances were in order. She may be feeling desperate."

"Kayla and desperation are a dangerous combination." Hunter threw the paper down in frustration.

"As terrible as she has been to Amber and me, I suspect she was only going along with her parents on her mother's orders."

"Which is why we decided not to press charges against her. Of course she doesn't know that."

"And might not even care if she did," Hunter added with a grimace.

Mr. Webb sighed.

"You'll have to tell Amber so that she doesn't get sideswiped with the story from somebody else. Hopefully, this will blow over. But I'm sure that there are other disreputable rags out there that want to make a quick buck off a sensationalized story. They won't care if they have the facts straight or not."

Mr. Webb folded the paper and passed it back across his desk.

Hunter groaned. He had a feeling Amber was going to take this hard. Anyone who spent five minutes around her would know that she wasn't the money hungry type of girl. He couldn't care less about what the tabloids said. This made no difference in wanting her as his wife. But he knew she wouldn't see it that clearly.

"She was staying home this morning anyway. Maybe I'll go and talk to her now."

"Good luck," Mr. Webb said, smiling at his son. "And remember, your mom and I don't care about these silly stories. Please let her know that we love her unconditionally."

"Thanks, Dad."

The more Hunter learned about Amber's parents, the more he appreciated his own. It drove him crazy that her past still haunted her. But he would do everything in his power to give her a better life than the one she grew up with.

Chapter 49

The waiting was the hard part. In spite of the tabloid story, Kayla still felt depressed. She had no way of knowing if Hunter, his family, or even Amber had seen the story. What if the story didn't even make it to that part of the world? Obviously, she hadn't thought this through.

The story had spread to a few other disreputable tabloid magazines. But the Webbs had been steadfastly silent, refusing to comment at all. In her fantasies, Kayla had imagined an indignant response from Hunter. But this was disturbing. This made it seem like they didn't care at all.

When not obsessively searching the internet for any pending gossip about the Webbs, Kayla was busy trying to present herself as a model. She was able to convince a guy from Higgins College to take some photographs of her that she could use for a portfolio. She hated not being able to hire a professional. But without cash, she didn't have any other option.

Once the photographs came in, she uploaded them to the link she had discovered earlier. The whole thing was a bit sketchy. Other than a basic website, the agency listed had no other presence that she could discover. But Kayla was getting anxious. If her ploy with the Webbs panned out, she had no idea what else she could do.

Richard432 was the one who asked her to upload her portfolio. He was also the one who contacted her back. It had taken a few days, but Kayla finally got a message from him saying that he had seen her photos and was interested in talking with her.

For the first time in a long time, Kayla felt a small thrill. She wasn't stupid enough to give out her address or phone number, but she was flattered. What would it hurt to meet him in a public place and see what he had to say?

She typed in a response, suggesting they meet at the local mall food court. If Richard, if that was indeed his real name, turned out to be a weirdo, she wouldn't feel trapped.

Less than ten minutes later, Richard responded, asking to meet the following day at noon. Kayla was both excited and leery at the same time. Was this guy sitting by his computer all day?

Of course, wasn't that what she was doing? Maybe he just kept his message box open at all times. At this point, Kayla didn't see what she had to lose. It wasn't like she had any other skills than her previous modeling stints for art class.

Moving through her house, Kayla hurried upstairs to her bedroom and entered her walk in closet. At least she had a generous wardrobe. The only issue was that she had packed on a few pounds this month from stress eating. It had been easy enough to hide a bit of a belly in a photo shoot with artfully arranged props.

But this was the real thing. She started to paw through the dresses and skirts. If looks alone were going to get her a job, she needed the right outfit.

Chapter 50

Amber was sitting on the living room sofa, making sketches for her next stained glass art project, when Hunter came home. She glanced at her watch, puzzled as to why he was so early.

"Hey! Is everything okay?"

Why was he staring at her with such a weird expression on his face?

Hunter ran his fingers through his hair before sitting down on the sofa next to her.

"I have something to tell you, but I don't want you to get upset."

Amber sat frozen. What could possibly have happened?

"First, I want you to know that I love you unconditionally. I wouldn't change one single thing about you."

Hunter stroked her cheek and smiled.

"I am so honored that you literally fell into my life at school."

"Hunter, what is it? What are you trying to tell me?"

Amber twisted her engagement ring nervously.

"And Mom and Dad feel the same. Dad said to tell you that specifically. They don't care about your past."

A chill passed over Amber. Her hands froze.

"What about my past? Just tell me before I go crazy."

Hunter sighed and reached over for his briefcase. Opening the latch, he removed a folded paper and handed it to Amber.

"Remember, this is just some trashy tabloid. They don't bother checking facts before they publish ridiculous stories.

It's the one where you find tales about UFO's and conspiracy theories."

Amber took the paper and stared in disbelief at the title.

MONEY CHASING STUDENT ABANDONS MOTHER TO WOO WEALTHY HEIR

There was a small photograph that must have come from her high school yearbook. Enlarging the picture had blurred the details. But still. It was her image plastered on the front page of a paper for all the world to see.

The other photograph, much larger, was apparently a recent one of her mother. Amber found her almost unrecognizable.

Hunter cleared his throat. "Dad and I think somebody put her up to this."

Amber turned to stare at him. "But why? And who? Hannah is still in rehab."

"We weren't thinking of Hannah," Hunter admitted. "More along the lines of Kayla Ross."

"But she doesn't even know my mother."

Amber stared down at the newspaper.

"None of this makes sense. Mom is crazy, but I can't see her going to the newspapers. She doesn't even know who you are."

Her brain tried to process the implications.

"Your family's reputation." Her hands flew to her mouth.

"Don't worry about that," Hunter said quickly. "And I mean that. Like I said, this is a trash publication and their reporters don't care about putting out the truth. It won't affect us."

He tried to pull away the paper, but Amber insisted on reading the small article inside. When she was finished reading about what a selfish, uncaring daughter she was, she burst into tears.

Everything was going so well. If this story spread, people would assume that she had gone after Hunter for his money.

Hunter yanked the paper from her hands, balled it up and threw it behind him.

"Don't you dare believe any of those stupid lies," he said roughly, taking her into his arms.

"I should have never brought that home."

But Amber couldn't get the headline out of her head. Was her fairy tale ending falling apart?

Chapter 51

Kayla got to the food court early. She smelled the cinnamon rolls baking nearby and found her mouth watering. But she couldn't afford to spend a couple of bucks on a snack. Besides, she now had to watch her waistline.

She wore sunglasses and a floppy hat that covered her face. Her table was partly hidden by a fake palm tree so that she could easily check out the people coming through without being easily seen herself. As she settled down to wait, she was surprised to hear a familiar voice. Turning to look behind her, she saw Mrs. Holloway and a man placing trays on a table several rows behind her.

"So, you just have the one son?" Mrs. Holloway asked in a sugary voice. "And he's all grown up and married now?"

Spinning in her seat, Kayla peeked from under the hat. Yes, definitely Mrs. Holloway. Apparently the idiot woman had assumed that the man would not see her picture in the paper.

"Yes, Peter lives in Ohio with his wife and two kids. And what about you? You said your husband died several years ago. Did you have any children?"

Kayla perked up her ears, eager to hear what the woman would say.

"No. I was never able to have children. It's just been me on my own all these years."

Her comment shocked Kayla. For the briefest moment, she had a sliver of sympathy for Amber. That moment passed quickly. Still, it took a special kind of maliciousness to deny that your own child even existed. Mrs. Holloway must have decided that she would more easily attract a man with no missing child to explain.

Kayla wasn't sure how she should handle this new development. Several days had passed and no other paper had picked up on the story. She had a feeling that her venture with Mrs. Holloway had been in vain. Now she had to hope that Richard was going to turn out to be her salvation.

Checking her phone, she saw that she only had a few more minutes before he was supposed to show up. Keeping her head low, she headed for the nearest restroom to check her appearance.

Beneath the floppy hat, Kayla's hair was perfectly waved. She wore a snug dress that emphasized her large breasts. An over-sized dark belt minimized the bit of belly she was starting to grow.

She knew she looked good. Most guys would appreciate her.

Except for Hunter. He never even looked twice.

A quick application of cherry red lipstick completed her look. Now this was something Kayla knew she could handle. Now to see if Richard, or whoever he might really be, was going to be someone she wanted to work with.

As she exited the restroom, she saw him almost immediately. He stood out starkly from most of the other patrons. Worldly. That was the look that Kayla thought of as she took in his tailored pants, silk shirt, and Italian shoes. Kayla knew her fashion and this man oozed luxury. She quickened her step.

As her heels clicked on the tiled floor, Richard looked up and appraised her with a small smile. He looked as though he liked what he saw.

"Kayla Ross, I presume?" He held out a soft, manicured hand as she approached.

His expensive cologne, one of her favorite's for men, wafted over her. He stared at her with deep blue eyes. His thick, glossy blonde hair was slicked back from his angular face.

Kayla thought she might swoon.

"And you are Richard . . . "

"Vogt. Richard Vogt. I'm delighted that you were able to meet with me on such short notice."

Kayla instantly regretted meeting this man here in a mall food court. She started to explain.

"I don't normally hang out in places like this, but . . ."

"But you wanted to make sure that you were safe in case I turned out to be a psychopath," Richard said, interrupting her.

"But unless you prefer to stay here, I know of a wonderful little restaurant where we can speak more comfortably."

Kayla's smile widened. "But of course!"

"Would you like to follow me? Or can I bring you back after our appointment?"

Kayla couldn't wait to see what kind of car Richard drove.

"Oh, just bring me back afterward. That gives us more time to get to know each other."

"My thoughts exactly." Richard's eyes focused on her chest.

Kayla didn't mind a bit. This looked like it could be the kind of relationship that kept her in the lifestyle she was born into.

She slid into the leather seat of his sports car as though she had every right to be there. Which she did. This is the life that she was supposed to lead. If all went well, Kayla hoped that she could leave Amber and Hunter behind.

The one thing that had always annoyed Kayla about Hunter was that he hid his wealth. Richard looked to have the same feeling as she did. Flaunt what you have.

Kayla hadn't been this happy in ages. Whether she got the job or not, she had a feeling that she already had Richard in the palm of her hands. At the very least, he would be a stepping stone to her future.

Chapter 52

Early afternoon sun poured through the large windows of the farmhouse bedroom. In a few hours, Amber would be married in the outdoor garden, surrounded by her new family and the few friends who had been invited to the private ceremony.

Amber stared at herself in the old-fashioned gilded mirror, feeling as though she was in the middle of a fairy tale. Even though she and Hunter had decided to have a very small, private wedding, no expense had been spared. Mrs. Webb insisted on taking Amber to some of the most exclusive shops to choose a wedding gown.

"No matter how big or how small the ceremony, your wedding day should be one that you always remember," her mother-in-law to be told her, unable to stop smiling.

"I've been dreaming about the day that Hunter gets married for a long time. Please let me have my fun."

Fun had included a day at an exclusive spa getting pampered like a princess. Amber's skin had been softened with seaweed wraps, her entire body given a gentle massage, a soothing manicure and pedicure, and her hair washed, dried and styled. Expert hands had skillfully applied light makeup to her face as she didn't want to look artificial on her special day.

Amber ultimately chose an elegant, close-fitting, flared lace gown with cap sleeves. Fortunately, the shop had her size right on the rack since there was no time to order anything. Only a few alterations to make up for her petite size were necessary.

Now here she sat with Hunter's mother and Madame Renaud fawning over her. Madame Renaud's husband had been teaching Amber the art of stained glass for several months. The childless couple had unofficially adopted Amber as their own.

"I took the liberty of wrapping Hunter's gift for you," Mrs. Renaud said shyly. "I hope that's okay."

"Oh, my gosh! I had totally forgotten about it!" Amber enveloped the woman in a grateful hug. "Thank you!"

"That reminds me," Hunter's mom said, intervening. "Hunter wants to exchange gifts before the ceremony if that's okay with you."

Mrs. Renaud nodded approving. "Oh, I think that's an excellent idea."

Amber smiled. "I think so too. I just hope that he likes my present."

"He would be crazy not to," Mrs. Renaud said. "Especially after all the effort you put into it."

Mrs. Webb chuckled.

"Now I'm intrigued myself. And I don't know what Hunter chose for you, either. I'm going to have twice the surprise factor."

Amber started to reply when there was a soft knock on the door.

"Is it okay for the photographer to come in now?" asked Mr. Webb.

"Absolutely!" Mrs. Webb hurried to the door.

Amber smiled as she heard Mrs. Webb speaking softly to her husband. Both the Webbs and the Renauds were such positive role models for married couples.

For the first time in her life, she felt truly loved and appreciated for who she was. Both families had filled in a gap her own mother had created. Amber wondered if she was simply selfish about being happy that her mother was excluded from this day. But she had no desire to even communicate with her birth mom. She was fortunate that both the Webbs and Renauds understood this.

Others in the past had chided her for not working to create a better mother-daughter relationship. What they didn't know was that Amber had always felt as though she was an unwelcome intrusion into her mother's life. And although that stung, she felt stronger for moving on. It helped that Madame Renaud and Hunter's mom were so supportive and loving.

After the photographer was finished, Amber and the two other women joined the others downstairs in the living room. Besides the Webbs and the Renauds, the other guests included: Pierre, the driver (and now a friend); Pierre's Uncle Gustav, the famous jewelry designer; Hunter's longtime best friend Caleb, and Megan (both a new friend as well as Caleb's girlfriend).

Amber shyly walked toward Hunter who was looking especially handsome in a dark suit with a silk tie.

Hunter's whole face lit up and he walked forward and clasped her hands.

"I want to kiss you right now," he whispered.

"And ruin my makeup?" Amber giggled. "I don't think so."

"I can't wait to give you your present," Hunter said, turning serious. "But you'll have to go back upstairs to find it."

"Okay . . ." Amber murmured. "Shall I go now?"

"Please."

With Mrs. Webb and Mrs. Renaud helping to protect the dress as she walked up the steps, Amber returned to the second floor of the farmhouse.

"Um . . . Where exactly am I going?"

"My old bedroom," Hunter called back.

Everyone was now crowded into the small hallway.

Amber opened the door and immediately gasped.

"Oh, Hunter! It's wonderful!"

She stepped into the room, mesmerized by the transformation. All of Hunter's childhood furniture had disappeared. Brand new easels stood by the bright window. One corner of the room held bins of colored glass. A worktable with locking wheels stood in another corner. Hanging shelves held brushes, paints, turpentine, glass cutters, coils of lead, and other art supplies.

"I know it's kind of small for an art studio. But I have plans to build a separate building at some point."

Hunter sounding anxious.

Amber swirled around, grabbed his shoulders, and kissed him fiercely.

"What about your makeup?" Hunter whispered when they finally broke for air.

"I'm not a big fan of makeup anyway," Amber said with a small sigh.

Behind them there was a clearing of throats.

Amber turned around sheepishly to laughter and clapping.

"There's a wedding scheduled downstairs," Mr. Webb said. "Let's not keep Monsieur le Curé waiting forever. I'm told he has pastoral obligations later this evening"

Amber took Hunter's hand as he led her downstairs and out into the garden with both Mrs. Webb and Mrs. Renaud stuck like glue to the train of the dress.

A canopy of white roses hung over them, perfuming the air as Amber exchanged vows with Hunter.

Amber felt as though she was floating. To stay grounded, she stared into Hunter's steady green eyes that sparkled like jewels.

She was only vaguely aware of what she was saying, now promising to cherish and love Hunter forever. She tried to remember each second but everything was moving so quickly.

And then, suddenly, Monsieur le Curé pronounced them man and wife and gave his blessing.

Hunter seized her in his arms and kissed her tenderly.

"Hello, Mrs. Webb," he said, pulling away at last and grinning.

"Hello, Mr. Webb," Amber replied, blushing. "I forgot to give you your gift earlier. Shall we work our way inside so that you can open it?"

After hugs and congratulations from everyone, they finally made their way back to the living room. While the guests enjoyed drinks and appetizers, Amber was able to pull Hunter aside for a moment of privacy.

"I kind of wanted you to open it up in private anyway," she said, nervously twisting the wedding band on her finger.

Hunter knelt and carefully removed the wrapping paper. Then he stared for a long time.

Amber suddenly doubted herself. What if he hated it?

But when Hunter turned to her, his eyes were filled with tears.

"It's perfect," he said, rising to his feet and kissing her again. "I want us to hang this where we can see it every day."

"Now, let's go show everyone how talented you are," he said briskly, carefully picking up the large stained glass piece.

Hunter carried the artwork outside in the bright garden.

Amber blushed as everyone gushed over her talent. She had created a portrait of herself and Hunter from broken pieces of colored glass, taking the pain from their fractured breakup and creating a beautiful image.

As she relished the attention and love poured out around her, she could think of only one word that described how she felt. Bliss.

****

Would you like more sweet romance?
Start reading *True Love*.

About True Love:

When college professor Amanda Evans meets Italian filmmaker Matteo Rosetti, she begins to entertain the notion. But Matteo is trapped in a complicated and manipulative relationship, enabled by his overbearing family. Despite all that is against them, Amanda and Matteo cannot deny the feelings they have for each other.

Romance blossoms, but is it enough for them to find a happily ever after? Even Matteo escaping his loveless relationship offers no guarantees. When all hope seems lost, can true love prevail?

Visit elliejadamsauthor.com for a
complete list of Sweet Romance books by Ellie.

Newsletter

Join my Newsletter and receive a Sweet Romance story as my gift to you. You will also receive author updates, new release alerts, and exclusive contests and discounts. Free to Join. No Spam. Unsubscribe Anytime. Join at www.elliejadamsauthor.com

Books by Ellie J. Adams

For a complete list of my Sweet Romance books, visit:
www.elliejadamsauthor.com

About the Author

Ellie J. Adams's books have been downloaded over half-a-million times by readers around the world. She is a romantic at heart and likes her characters to find their Happily Ever After. Ellie's books offer moments of drama, humor, and heartache along the way. Her leading men are strong, but flawed, males, and the leading women are sweet, smart, and independent. Ellie writes sweet romance you can get swept up in and takes you away.

www.ingramcontent.com/pod-product-compliance
Lightning Source LLC
Chambersburg PA
CBHW050343190726
48284CB00007BB/2125